C000226131

BORN OF EARTH

AN ELEMENTAL ORIGINS NOVEL

A.L. KNORR

Edited by

TERESA HULL

INTELLECTUALLY PROMISCUOUS PRESS, 2017

❀ Created with Vellum

ALSO BY A.L. KNORR

The Elemental Origins Series

Born of Water

Born of Fire

Born of Earth

Born of Aether

Born of Air

The Elementals

Pyro, A Fire Novella

The Wreck of Sybellen

The Kacy Chronicles

Descendant

Ascendant

Combatant

Transcendant

Anthologies & Boxed Sets

Sirens & Scales

Join A.L. Knorr's VIP Reader List and she'll personally send you a reminder as soon as her next book is out. Visit alknorrbooks.com to sign up.

When the unclean spirit is gone out of a man, he walketh through dry places, seeking rest; and finding none, he saith, I will return unto my house when I came out. And whence he cometh, he findeth it swept and garnished. Then goeth he, and taketh to him seven other spirits more wicked than himself; and they enter in, and dwell there: and the last state of that man is worse than the first.

Luke 11: 24-25

PROLOGUE

I have never been a diary kind of girl. Yet here I sit, laptop open, fingers flying. I'm imagining you are my future child or grandchild, it helps to think we're related and that maybe these words will help you.

It's the end of the most mind-blowing, amazing, disruptive, life-changing summer of my life. I am not sure how I could have understood the happenings and changes I faced these past two months without the scribblings of an ancestor. And with that, I have become… a diary girl.

In a few days, I'll see my best friends - friends who have become my family. I haven't decided how to tell them what happened to me, who I've become, what I am. I'm still trying to figure that out myself. I don't want to spook them, especially with what I've learned about Saltford, our hometown. I guess I'll worry about that when time comes. For now, I'm going back. Back to the evening I last saw them, and back to a place of blissful ignorance.

CHAPTER 1

I closed the front door and leaned against it, sighing. Alone again. Our gigantic foyer echoed with the sound of my footsteps as I crossed the marble expanse in my Jimmy Choo flip flops, past our restaurant-sized but mostly un-used kitchen, through our quadruple sliding patio doors and into our perfectly-kept-by-complete-strangers back yard.

I dumped the melted ice from four used iced-tea glasses, stacked them, and folded the blankets, still warm from the bodies of my best friends - Targa, Saxony, and Akiko. My friends were gone for the summer. Our goodbyes had been said.

These are the girls who know that all it takes to make me cry is a video of a horse running in slow motion - I'm not kidding - the waterworks just start. These are the girls who know how to get me laughing so hard I get cramps. These are the girls who know that I left anonymous love-notes inside Gregory Handler's shoe in Grade 4.

A hollow feeling buckled my knees. The familiar metallic glint of loneliness soured in my mouth and I plopped down in one of the deck chairs. The dark sky, so beautiful in its star-speckled glory while my friends were here, now looked like it was going to swallow me in its cold gaping maw. I stared into the dying embers. The insects had stopped singing and the fire had run out of heat. Silence stuffed my ears in one of those moments where you wonder if you've actually gone deaf. The dwindling fire gave a snap and confirmed I hadn't lost my hearing, just my besties for the summer.

The grinding hum of our garage door alerted me that Liz was home. Liz was about to get some happy news. Targa's last-minute opportunity to go to Poland with her mom meant that I'd be leaving, too. Decision made. Ireland, here I come. I hadn't been planning on leaving. It had been twelve years since I'd been to visit my Aunt Faith, she's practically a stranger. Then again, so is Liz. So what's the difference? Stay home in Saltford with my laptop? Or get on a plane and visit the Emerald Isle for the summer?

I loaded my arms with the blankets and took them inside. "Liz?" I closed the patio door behind me with my toes.

"In here, Poppet," she answered from her home office, in her manufactured aristocratic English accent. *Poppet.* Why is it that when a term of endearment isn't delivered with any actual affection it sounds like you're calling over a barnyard animal? Perhaps a piglet?

Liz should have an Irish accent, like my Aunt Faith does, but not long after she made partner she took classes to train herself to sound British. Why? No idea. Maybe she thinks legalese comes out better in an English accent.

I dumped the smoky blankets in the laundry hamper and padded down our plushly-carpeted hallway, silent as a panther. I swear you could drop a dead body down our stairs and you wouldn't hear a thing. Targa takes off her socks just so she can feel the thick softness of our carpet with her toes. I can't bring myself to do the same, I hate the feeling of bare feet. My soles are too sensitive. Every little piece of dirt, pokey bit of carpet, or blade of grass feels magnified.

"Hey," I poked my head into Liz's office. She was already pecking away rapid-fire on her laptop, a stack of file folders at her right hand, her Prada bifocals perched on the end of her nose. Her hair looked like it hadn't budged since she left at 5:45 on the nose this morning. "Got a minute?"

"Just. What is it?" She didn't look up from the keyboard, and her fingers flew faster if that was possible. Any moment now, they could start smoking.

"I'm going to go to Ireland for the summer. Like you wanted."

That got her attention. She looked up. Lines creased her forehead as she peered over her glasses, her bionic fingers momentarily paused. "You are? What happened, I thought you and Targa were going to hang out, camp, that sort of thing. Isn't that what you said last week? I'm sure that's what you said."

Camp? I hate camping. Seriously?

She took off her glasses and put the end bit in her mouth. I could see the gears turning, the drawers of files opening and closing in her mind as she searched for the most up to date information. "Did you and Targa have a falling out?"

Targa and I never fight. If Liz had ever observed us together or ever asked me anything about my best friend, she'd know that.

"No. Targa is going to Poland, last minute decision. No point in me hanging about the house by myself all summer. I thought you'd be happy." I stepped inside and sat in one of the two matching leather chairs facing her desk, like a client. I crossed my ankles and folded my hands in my lap. Might as well play the part, make her feel at home. My physical sarcasm was lost on her.

"I am happy, Poppet. That's great. Call Denise on Monday and she'll set you up with flights. She's updated your passport already, so you're good to go." She put her glasses on and attacked her keyboard again. Denise is Liz's secretary. She makes sure I don't miss a dental cleaning, a haircut or a manicure (I don't do pedicures. Ugh). They all happen like clockwork. Thanks, Denise.

"Are you going to talk to Aunt Faith? I mean, she already said I can come, right?"

Liz didn't look up. "Yes, Poppet. She's good with it. Denise will settle everything with her next week. She'll even pick you up from the train station. Faith, not Denise, obviously." Liz was especially adept at clarity-to-go. I think it's a lawyer thing.

"I have to take a train?"

"Fly to Dublin, train to Anacullough. You don't remember?" *Type. Type. Type.*

"I was five."

"Denise will explain, it's easy. Ireland's public transport is excellent."

"Excellent." I watched her type. I cleared my throat.

She blinked up at me, then back down. "You'll have fun. Jasher will be there too, your cousin. You'll have a friend to play with."

Wow. Did she really just say that I'd have a friend to play with? What was I, three?

"What's he like?"

She frowned. "I don't know, never met him. You know that. I'm sure he's lovely."

"Well, how old is he? I know he's older than me but by how much? What does he do? Is he a baseball kind of guy, or a movie-buff?"

She blinked. I'd bewildered her with these questions about her adopted nephew. She wasn't prepared. She hated not being prepared. "Ah," she said, holding up a finger. She opened one of her many desk drawers. Rummaged. Closed the drawer. Opened another one. Rummaged. She pulled out a stack of envelopes wrapped with an elastic band. She plopped them on the edge of her desk with a thwack and set her shoulders back triumphantly. "There you are."

"What are these?" I crossed the expanse to her desk and picked up the stack of letters. Elegant handwritten scrawl. Postmarked from Ireland.

"Letters from your Aunt Faith. Once you've read those you'll know everything I know about Jasher, and you'll be all caught up on the goings on over there." She waved her fingers as though doing a spell. Embarrassment over her lack of information, magically averted.

"Looks like I'll know *more* than you, Liz. Half of these aren't even open." I thumbed through the stack.

"Good!" She looked up and flashed me one last winning smile.

"Good," I echoed. I stood there for a moment, bathing in the sound of typing. In her mind, I was gone already. "Okay, I'm going to go numb myself with technology now."

She glanced up as briefly as blinking. "Okay, Poppet. Have fun."
I left, the carpet muffling the sound of my exit.

CHAPTER 2

My room looked like a bomb had gone off. I was sitting on my bedroom floor, suitcase open, stacks of clothes around me sitting in 'yes', 'no', and 'maybe' piles. I kept checking the weather in Ireland and trying to pack appropriately. So far all I had learned was that Irish weather in summer was as predictable as the stock market. Layers it would be.

The stack of letters on my dresser caught my eye. I had packing fatigue anyway, so I pushed myself up from cross-legged, unfolding myself on what Saxony called my stork legs. I grabbed the stack and went to make a cappuccino from our one-of-a-kind espresso machine. Liz had imported it from Naples. It looks like a spaceship.

I sat in our bright, airy kitchen, with only the sound of the ticking clock for company. I took a sip of my frothy drink and pulled the elastic off the stack of letters. The rubber band broke, snapping against my fingers. These letters must have been in that drawer for a while. At least Liz was kind enough to stack them chronologically before she hid them away from the light for all eternity. I shook my head as I shuffled through the letters, the majority with unbroken seals. No wonder Faith had stopped writing. Why bother?

There was no word of Jasher until several letters in. So far, it was mostly about her work as a nurse and then her struggles with the medical establishment, her desire to change occupations. She espoused a strong wish to bring together modern technology and 'ancient wisdom,' as she called it.

I came across a photograph of the property in Ireland. It looked exactly as I remembered. The Victorian house that Faith and Liz referred to as Sarasborne was old but well kept, white with sage trim. There was something regal about that house. The yard was severely manicured - topiaries perfectly trimmed, closely clipped grass, well-pruned shrubs and carefully monitored borders of domestic flowers in alternating colors. According to Liz, my grandmother Roisin (pronounced *Rosheen*) had been a clean-freak inside the house, and my grandfather Padraig (*Patrick*) had been a rabid gardener on the outside, wielding his control over nature like a dictator. It showed in the organized perfection of every detail of the yard. The date on the back of the photo was 2000, the year after I'd been born and the year my grandfather had passed away. Our family had been whole at that point and we had gone to Ireland together for the funeral. I don't remember anything about the trip. The next time we'd gone was for my grandmother's funeral. I had never gotten to know my grandparents very well, but I was sufficiently grief-stricken for the visit because my dad had just abandoned us. Liz and Brent had divorced but agreed on joint custody. Turned out my dad didn't even want that, because in less than a year he was gone in a puff of cigarette smoke, leaving only a cell phone number for emergencies. Liz was never the same. She tried to be a good mom, for a while. We did pretty well together until I was eleven. But then she started making real headway at work, made partner, and that, as they say, was that.

I scanned more letters: Faith offering moral support to Liz, inviting her to come back and live at home. Suggesting they could raise me together in Ireland. She admitted to being lonely, to having a few suitors but none were 'the one.'

Leaning against the kitchen counter, I was feeling drowsy when Faith finally wrote something interesting about witnessing a medical miracle. A patient had died in childbirth, but the baby had been saved.

Never have I seen such a thing, she wrote. *By all that is medically sound, this child should not be alive. His father christened him Jasher.*

There he was - the first mention of my adopted cousin. If he had a father, how did he end up with my aunt? I read on, supposing that a tragedy had claimed his dad as well. But there was no mention of Jasher for the next several years. I scanned, looking for his name.

The next letter dumped two photographs into my lap. The first was of Faith squatting on the lawn and holding a small boy in her lap. On the back of the photograph was written *Faith & Jasher, summer 2006.* I studied the boy. He was lean and lanky, dark skinned, dark eyed, and dark haired. In spite of all the sun he was obviously getting, he looked like someone had just shot his puppy. Haunted expression. No smile. Circles of sleeplessness under his eyes.

The second photograph was of Jasher alone. A little older, he was standing next to a fountain. Taller, still scrawny, and still with those tortured eyes.

I know you'll be shocked to your core, Liz. But I've taken the decision to adopt Jasher. His father never really recovered from the loss of Maud, and seems now incapable (by his own admission) of raising the lad. He and I have yet to settle the paperwork, which will be arduous, but Jasher is already living with me, and seems to be in better spirits. Faith's tone was formal, always skimming the surface.

I continued to read, sniffing for clues like a hound. Jasher had a hard time in school in Anacullough. He didn't make friends easily. He wasn't sleeping, and he faced every day with dread. Faith finally took him out of school for a year and hired a tutor to home-school him while she continued to work. She wrote that Jasher's health improved after that, and he slept better and seemed happier. She admitted to being concerned about his reclusive tendencies, as he never liked to go anywhere. He was always outdoors, working in the yard, but he didn't like to leave the property.

I finally hit the last letter in the stack. My eyes were taken by a picture of a fairy on the back of the envelope. It had yellow hair and yellow wings that looked damp and crinkled. I peered closer, and ran the pad of my thumb over it. The drawing had been done by hand, probably with pencil crayons, and it was very well done. The little fae face was sleepy and realistic, not cartoonish in any way. Interesting. Faith had some artistic skill.

What I had learned so far was that Jasher was a social recluse but as he had grown, he had found his stride. He had a taste for horticulture, landscaping, and carpentry. He was as outdoorsy as they come. Faith's words in the last letter oozed with motherly pride. Another photograph fell out from between the two pages and landed face down on the floor. Scrawled on the back in Faith's neat handwriting was *Jasher Sheehan, Summer 2013*. He was officially sporting the name Sheehan. In 2013, he would have been sixteen. I picked the photo up and turned it over.

I'd like to think that I can see deeper than a pretty face, but I'll admit that I dropped an inadvertent 'Holy wow.' Faith and Jasher posed in front of a wooden gazebo, his arm around her shoulders. For the first time, there was a smile on his face. The man in the photograph looked like a completely different person than the boy in earlier letters. He towered over Faith. He wore a plain white t-shirt and a pair of jeans. Bare feet poked out from under the frayed denim hems. His shoulders stretched the fabric of his shirt. The other arm not around Faith's shoulders was propped over the railing of the gazebo. A tanned hand curled around one of the posts, the fingers square and the nails bluntly cut. A baseball cap turned backward covered thick brown curls and his head was tilted up toward the light. His dark eyes were half closed. His grin and white teeth shone starkly from his tanned face. The shadow of a black beard played about his jaw. He looked twenty-five, not sixteen. He looked like a toothpaste ad, not a hermit. He looked like a hale and hearty farm boy, not a recluse.

This was the guy I'd be spending the summer with? I gulped. He was too perfect for words.

This photograph was three years old already. What was he like now? Leaving out the most recent photo of Jasher and Faith, I stacked the letters as they had been. I found a fresh elastic to bind them. After throwing them into Liz's office drawer, I went back to my room. I tucked the photo into the corner of my corkboard and looked at it thoughtfully. I was swept through by a desire to know these people, and maybe figure out why my mom had distanced herself from her family so much.

Knowing Liz, Faith would have not had a single reply to any of those letters. Maybe a couple of the early ones, but certainly none since she'd made partner. If Faith was lucky, she would have received a digital Christmas card...but that's about it.

Jasher knew I existed for sure, but he'd know hardly anything about me. How did he feel about having his cousin come and stay with them for the summer? Was he still painfully shy, the way Faith had described him in his youth? Would we get along?

I turned back to my packing. I picked up a pretty teal summer dress which I had tossed into the 'no' pile because I thought it was more for a tropical destination. I held it up thoughtfully. It did look cute on me, maybe even sexy. I folded it and put it on the 'yes' pile.

CHAPTER 3

I stepped off the train and onto the warm stone platform at the Anacullough station. The air was humid and rich with the smells of green things. I rolled my luggage out of the way of the sliding door to make sure I wasn't blocking passengers wanting to get off. Then I noticed that I was, in fact, the only passenger getting off the train.

A bright shaft of sunlight slanted down between the train and platform roof. I pulled my sunglasses out of my purse and propped them on top of my head. Apparently, I'd need them. Sun in Ireland, who knew? I folded the rain jacket I had been carrying and stuffed it into the front pocket of my carry-on.

Ana's station was a cute, old-fashioned affair with lacquered iron benches and matching iron posts, wrought with leaves of ivy. Except for a roof overhanging the platform, the station was open to the air. A delicious breeze smelling of freshly cut grass lifted the hair gently away from my forehead.

I looked around for Aunt Faith. A man sat on a bench hiding his face behind a newspaper. A station employee swept dust, gum wrappers and dead leaves into a portable dustbin. No Aunt Faith yet. I took a deep breath and stretched the stiffness from my hips.

I remembered my promise to Targa, Saxony, and Akiko and pulled out my cell phone to fire off a text to the group. Saxony was in Italy already, so that put her an hour ahead of me. Akiko was in transit to Kyoto, and Targa was in Poland, so also an hour ahead of me. I tapped out a text to the group.

Middle of nowhere. Irish country-side. Population - Me, some ruins, a lot of green stuff, and a bunch of old farts who talk weird.

Targa wrote back almost immediately: *Glad you've arrived alive, now stop complaining and enjoy it.*

Saxony's response came in a few minutes later: Well lookee who it is. Send me pix of your cousin or ur dead meat.

Me: *Adopted cousin.*

Saxony: *Whatevs. I want a shot of him cleaning the pool, please. Thank you. That is all. Now go away. Do you have any idea how early it is here?*

Me: *Isn't it lunchtime?*

Saxony: *Exactly. Shoo.*

Me: *LOL. Gone.*

I snapped my phone case shut and slipped my phone into the front pocket of my purse.

"Georjayna?" A soft, Irish-accented voice startled me from behind.

I jumped, clutching my chest with one hand and catching my sunglasses with the other as they slid off my head. "Sweet baby Jane!"

My aunt looked exactly the way I remembered her. A wide grin sandwiched between soft cheeks and a kerchief covering her curly blond hair. She reached up to hug me and I caught of whiff of something herbal and pleasant.

"I didn't mean to startle you," she said. Her Irish lilt was music to my ears. "Heavens! You're so..."

"Tall?"

"I was going to say bonny, but yes, that too. How was your journey?"

"Good, thanks." We made our way to her hybrid vehicle as we got all of the niceties out of the way. I'd taken to staring at the thick foliage swallowing station. I had forgotten just how lush and green Ireland really was. You don't tend to notice these things when you're a kid. I folded myself into the passenger seat, my knees jutting up as high as the glove compartment. I closed the door, cracked the passenger window, and inhaled.

"Do you mind if we nip to the market on our way home? I need a few things," Faith asked as she turned on the car. It was so quiet I couldn't even tell it was running.

"Not at all."

"I might as well let you know right away," Faith said. "I'm taking a course in Aberdeen for a couple of weeks at the end of July. You and Jasher should know each other pretty well by then. Think you'll be okay on your own? I already told your mom and she said you're used to being on your own." Her mouth pulled down just a little.

"Yeah, I am. No worries, Auntie. I'm sure we'll be fine. What's the course about?"

"It's a reflexology course. I studied it nearly a decade ago. I need a refresher."

"Last time I was here, you worked as a nurse, right?"

"That's right."

"What do you do now?"

"Oh, I'm still a health care practitioner, but I transitioned out of nursing and into holistic care. Herbology, some meridian work, but mainly reflexology. I guess your mom never told you."

"What's reflexology?"

"It's a therapy that uses the reflex points in the body. By applying pressure and stimulating these points, I can help someone to heal. Mostly through points in the feet." She looked over at me, her eyes lit. "Did you know that your feet are a gateway to the rest of your body? It's really good for you to walk in the grass and dirt in bare feet, all the energy and helpful bacteria in the soil boosts our health."

Helpful bacteria? I squirmed in the passenger seat. "I didn't know that, Auntie," I said politely. The last thing I'd be doing was rooting around in the dirt in bare feet. Just the thought made me want to pull my sensitive feet up underneath me and swaddle them in bubble wrap.

Faith slowed the car as we entered town. "Here we are." She pulled into a parking space in front of a grocery market. "Want to come in with me?"

"Sure." I unbuckled my seat belt. "I've been sitting too much anyway."

I followed my aunt through the market, scanning the gossip rags and fashion magazines. Faith was through the checkout with her bag of groceries quickly as there were no other customers.

We headed out into the street and nearly bumped into a huge man in a black newsboy cap. A loaf of bread fell out of Faith's bag.

"Scuse me," said the man as he bent to pick up the bread. He held it out for Faith, and for a moment, it seemed like she wasn't going to take it. I looked at her curiously, but couldn't read her expression. She seemed a little paler than usual.

"Ta," Faith said finally, taking the bread. "How are you, Brendan?"

"Good as can be expected," he said. Brendan had a close-cropped gray beard and marionette lines bordering his mouth. He nodded at me.

"Did I hear rightly?" Faith asked. "You bought the old O'Brien place?"

"News travels fast," Brendan answered in a thicker accent than Faith's. "I did."

My aunt visibly paled. "I had hoped it was just a rumor."

"The price was right." He said it a bit sharply, I thought.

"I imagine so," Faith said, half under her breath. "Are you planning to live there?"

"Of course, why else would I have purchased it? I can't live in my ma's spare room for the rest of my life."

I hoped I hid my surprise well. The man looked well dressed and at least mid-fifties. Why was he living in his mother's house?

"I know, but...there's bad energy there, Brendan. You can tell just from looking."

I looked at Faith, intrigued. Liz had always quashed the notion of good or bad energy, but if I were pushed to say what I believed? Well, it was easy to feel that the energy between Liz and me wasn't so much on the positive side any more. So, bad energy? Sure. I knew what that meant.

"I don't go in for all that nonsense, you know that," he groused. "It just needs some fertilizer and some proper care. It's been neglected for seventy-some years."

"When do you take possession?" Faith asked, hiking the groceries. I reached to take the bag from her and she gave me a grateful smile.

"Two weeks," Brendan said, already moving away from us.

"I see." Faith looked as though she didn't see at all, not a bit.

"Well, I'll be on my way." He put a fingertip to the brim of his cap and went into the store.

"Who was that, Auntie?" I asked, opening the door to the hybrid.

She sighed and opened the driver's side door. "No one you need to know, Sweetpea."

A word to the wise: When someone says somebody is no one you need to know...you probably need to know.

CHAPTER 4

Twelve years ago, the large Victorian house was bare and stark white with fresh paint. Now it was buried in foliage. A small wooden sign with the words *Sara Rugadh* above and *Sarasborne* below greeted us at the corner as Faith steered the car into the driveway.

"What's Sarasborne?" I asked Faith, not bothering to try and pronounce the Gaelic version.

"It's quite literal. The first child born in this house was Sara Sheehan, in 1823. If the story is to be believed," she added with a laugh, "the house wasn't even finished before the wee thing made her appearance. She came with so little warning that there was no time to shoo the workmen. She was born amid the sounds of hammers and saws. *Sara Rugadh* means 'born before.'

"Two hundred years of ancestry," I said, more to myself as I stared up at the huge structure. And I hardly knew a thing about my family.

"Yes, this place has a lot of history," said Faith.

Greenery crawled over every surface. Windows peeked out from between thick curtains of ivy. A three-car garage stood alone and it, too, was buried in a tangle of vines and leaves. Little white and orange flowers dotted the side of it. It was Ireland, over-jacked on chlorophyll.

Faith pulled the car into the garage and killed the engine. I got out with some difficulty - I swear cars in Ireland are smaller. I walked out of the garage and looked around, struck. A stone terrace coming off the rear of the house was lined with arches dripping with purple blossoms. Fronds hung down in elegant cones like fragrant chandeliers. The perfume of flowers filled the air.

"Wow," I said as my eyes scanned Sarasborne. "I've never seen a house that looks like nature is holding it up more than timbers and beams." A small pond containing koi and green buds that promised to become flowers sparkled next to the terrace where wicker patio furniture had been arranged on the flagstones. Beyond that was the gazebo made from iron gray barn board. It too would be swallowed up with greenery soon. Already ivy was creeping up the bottoms of every post.

"Do you like it?" Faith came to stand beside me.

"As long as there are no bees, I love it," I said.

Faith gave me a puzzled look.

I cleared my throat. My phobia was an embarrassing topic. "It's beautiful. Did Jasher make that?" I asked, pointing to the gazebo.

"He built everything, except for the house of course. He was cleaning away an old barn for one of his landscaping projects and the fellow allowed him to take whatever was worthy of being reclaimed. He made the gazebo over a weekend. Marvelous, isn't it?"

I nodded. "It all looks so wild and alive."

Faith laughed. "Your grandparents would have used the word 'wild,' too. I think they'd turn over in their graves to see it now." She popped open the trunk and pulled out my luggage. I went to help. "After Mum and Dad passed away, I just let things go, preferring to let nature take its course. Now, Jasher at least keeps the yard mowed." She closed the trunk and picked up my carry-on bag. "Let's get you settled."

"Where is this mysterious cousin-in-law of mine?" I asked, rolling my suitcase along the flagstone path.

"He's at work. He'll be home a little later. He's almost always done by three."

Good. I could take a nap. Tendrils of ivy grazed the top of my head as I ducked inside the house. Just beyond the mudroom was the kitchen. An intoxicating herbal scent filled the air. "What's that smell?"

She gave me a look of disbelief. "You don't recognize the scent of lavender?" She pointed to a potted plant on the breakfast table in the nook. Spikes of purple flowers topped a cluster of small-leafed stems. "Honestly, has your mother taught you nothing about healing herbs? She and I grew up using herbs. I'm surprised she didn't pass on that knowledge to you."

"Nope." I couldn't say I'd ever been interested, either. "Smells great though," I said as we shuffled past the kitchen with my bags.

She took me up to the room on the second floor that had once belonged to Liz. Situated at the rear corner of the house, it overlooked the backyard. Like most of the rooms in Victorian houses, it was huge and had its own fireplace. A worn carpet protected the hardwood floor and a four-poster bed was the centerpiece of the room. An antique writing desk sat under one of the three large windows, the perfect place to do my coursework.

I'd signed up for an online course in photo composition. I'd always enjoyed snapping photos and had even won a competition with a shot I'd taken of Targa down at the beach one summer. She'd been running into the ocean but looking back at me, her dark hair flying. A wave had hit her in the thighs, framing her body with white spray which sparkled in the sunshine. She looked like a fantasy creature.

Faith set my carry-on down and turned to me. "Now, I know you're bit of a technology fiend..."

"Did Liz tell you that?"

"She did. I think your mom was worried that you'd shrivel up and die without the internet." She winced. "But we don't have wifi in this house."

My face froze. "Seriously?" I remember thinking that Liz must have been afraid to tell me, afraid I wouldn't have gone. I couldn't picture life without wifi.

"I know it's hard to believe." Faith put her palms up. "But you'll find that the Ana County Library and most of the cafes in town have wifi."

"You and Jasher don't use the internet?" I asked, bemused. "How do you survive?" This was insanity in my world. I had just assumed, well, didn't *everyone* have wifi these days?

She laughed. "Oh Georjie, there is so much to be done, we don't have time for it."

"But don't you use it for research? For email? For your work? Liz gave me your phone number. It's a cell, isn't it?"

"Yes, I'm not a complete dinosaur. I do have a mobile. For wifi, you can use my bicycle and go into town whenever you wish. There's a path, it's quite pretty and it only takes a few minutes to get to the main square."

"Um, okay. Thanks," I said, already strategizing to mitigate the damage. I'd have to make a hotspot with my cell. There was no way I would bike into town every time I needed wifi.

"I'm going to work in my office for the afternoon," Faith said, resting her hand on the door handle. "Then I've got an appointment in town. I'll see you tonight."

Faith left me alone and I rifled through my luggage for my sleep shorts. Combing and then braiding my long, travel-matted hair, I stood at the window to look out over the beautiful green yard and admire the Eden.

I blinked as two tiny and brightly colored tracers flew by my window at light speed. I stepped closer and peered through the warped glass in the direction they'd gone. No dice. They'd vanished. I yawned and rubbed my dry eyes. Must have been hummingbirds. I crawled between the cool clean sheets and enjoyed the sleep of the blissfully ignorant.

CHAPTER 5

When I woke from my nap, Aunt Faith was gone, but she'd left a covered tray of food on the kitchen counter with a sticky note and my name scrawled in her fine penmanship. To my delight, a fresh scone with clotted cream, fruit preserves, and a couple of hard-boiled eggs had been artfully arranged on a china set. I fumbled around the large kitchen looking for tea and trying to make the gas stove work. I emerged triumphant with a cup, and took my laptop and tray of eats out to the gazebo. My flip flops thwacked against the bottoms of my feet as I walked the stone path Jasher had made, rendering the birds temporarily silent.

I settled myself at the table in the gazebo and set my laptop, e-reader, and cell phone out in front of me. This almost fit my idea of heaven. At least I could use photoshop or read without needing wifi.

The scone melted in my mouth. It's a simple thing, and maybe not worthy of note, but at home I ate a lot of sandwiches and microwave dinners. Even with our architectural-digest-worthy kitchen, Liz was allergic to cooking and I considered it an achievement to toast bread without burning it.

I had just finished my tea when I heard a vehicle pull into the driveway. It had to be Jasher because Faith's hybrid was nearly silent.

The engine died and the door opened and closed. A squeaky tailgate was lowered, followed by scraping noises. Butterflies spiraled through my stomach, much to my annoyance. Why was I so nervous? I told myself it had nothing to do with how handsome he was in the photographs I'd seen—I wasn't that shallow, was I?

Jasher appeared around the corner, and my breath caught in my chest.

There have been moments in my life when seeing someone for the first time gives me the strangest sensation. Trying to define the feeling makes it vaporize. It's like seeing something in my periphery, but when I look, there's nothing there.

It hasn't happened too many times in my life, just a couple. Targa's Mom, Mira, still does it to me. Not every time I see her, but every once in a while when I least expect it, the feeling blows through me like smoke through grass.

I could now add Jasher to my short list of people who give me this feeling.

He was even taller than he'd appeared in the photograph, not to mention broader and browner from hours spent outside. He hadn't seen me yet. Should I call out a hello or to wait until he spotted me? My tongue decided for me and sat frozen in my mouth.

Jasher carried a collection of window frames that looked like he'd rescued them from the dump. Most of the panes of glass were broken. He propped them against the side of the garage and disappeared from view. More scraping sounds. He reappeared with another load of the same.

I couldn't see his features well from the distance but I could see the slashes of dark eyebrows and eyelashes and ruddy cheeks through several days' worth of beard growth. He wore a black t-shirt and baggy tan shorts made of canvas that reached his knees. He would have made a good cover model for a men's health mag.

Thinking of Saxony, I grabbed my phone and opened my camera. I zoomed in on him and took a photo just before he deposited another load of windows. I winced at the digital capture noise, which I hadn't turned off.

He looked up, shielding his eyes from the late afternoon sun. I tucked my phone beside my laptop. He grinned and my heart did a little flip. *Holy supernova smile.*

"Hello!" he called. His voice was like melted caramel. Cheesy I know, but I'm trying to be honest here.

"Hi," I called back. I twirled a lock of hair with my fingers, realized it, and abruptly dropped my hand. What was I doing? I had never allowed a handsome face to vaporize my self-possession. Why did I suddenly feel like I was twelve? Boys were supposed to be the awkward ones, not me.

He crossed the lawn, taking his work gloves off. The beauty of his features became clearer. He was all eyelashes and cheek bones and white teeth and good grief. A finely made man like that doesn't have to try very hard to provoke a physical reaction in a woman. He had a pleasant, open expression and an easy grin, but as he approached something strange happened. His eyes fell on the array of technology in front of me and his smile disappeared. A second dose of that strange sensation whispered past.

“What are you doing?” he demanded.

"Just doing a bit of work. I signed up for a summer course," I said. It was a lie, I had been eating a scone, not working, but for some reason I felt like I should explain myself. Why did I feel defensive?

His dark eyes went from my laptop to my e-reader to my cell phone and a look of annoyance crossed his face. He held his gloves in his hands.

In an effort to shatter the film of ice that had formed between us for reasons I didn't understand, I stood and held out my hand. "Nice to finally meet you, Jasher."

He looked at my hand as if I was offering him a snake carcass on a fork instead of a handshake. Finally, he stepped forward, reached over the gazebo railing and took my fingers in his big calloused ones. The warmth from his touch rolled up my arm. He pumped my hand once and then let go quickly. A cold draft swept over me. He gave a stiff nod but didn't say anything. Then he tapped his gloves against his palm. "Well, I've got work to do. Enjoy your course."

Did I imagine it, or had he said *course* with barely contained disdain? He strode back toward his truck and disappeared around the corner of the house. The truck door opened and closed. When he reappeared, he was wearing a baseball cap and safety glasses. He didn't look at me again. He went about setting up sawhorses in front of the garage and preparing to do goodness knew what with all those windows. I felt completely idiotic.

After his cold reception, I couldn't focus. He was right there, ignoring me. I packed my things into my laptop bag and went into the house. I was so confused that all I did was pace in my room for about five full minutes. What was his problem? I hadn't been hurting anyone. If this was how it was going to be between us, then I may as well pack up and go home. The summer stretched out in front of me, endless and uncomfortable.

The day was too nice and I couldn't focus anyway, so I grabbed my phone and went back outside. I thought I'd take some pictures while the light was nice. Photography always made me feel better. I wandered the opposite direction of the garage, keeping my distance from Jasher. He was working and not paying me any mind. I doubted he even knew that I'd left in the first place.

I took pictures of the pond and the gazebo and scanned Sarasborne's yard. A thickly forested area lined the back of the property, and I could make out a small bridge arching a stream. A narrow break in the trees showed hilly fields beyond, with a walking path leading off into the bush. As I was taking a 360-degree panoramic photo, my eye caught on something attached to the side of the house that I hadn't noticed before. A greenhouse.

It was made out of an assortment of mismatched old windows of all shapes and sizes. Amazed, I went closer. So this was what Jasher was doing with all those old windows. I hadn't noticed it before because it was hidden around the far side of the house. It was enormous. Even with an untrained eye I could see that this building was a marvel. How Jasher had managed to piece together such a greenhouse using only old windows was a mystery to me. Impressed, I looked over at Jasher. He had his head down over his workbench and a window under his clever hands.

I approached the greenhouse, taking in the details. It was attached to Sarasborne. There must have been an entrance inside, coming off one of the rooms. Maybe there was a parlor at that end of the house? I couldn't recall.

The footprint of the building was a simple key-shape. The round part had a large domed roof. The neck of the key was a narrow column that connected to Sarasborne. A blur of greenery was all I could make out through the glass. Most of the panes were old and warped. Towards the top of the dome, the branches of some enterprising tree poked out. Maybe that was what Jasher was fixing.

I took some photos of the greenhouse. It had to be unique the world over. As I stepped closer, I was startled by an angry, "Hey!"

My head snapped up. Jasher was looking at me, his brows drawn together to form an angry line between his eyes. I looked behind me and around my feet, trying to work out what he was upset about. I wasn't standing in any delicate shrubs or anything.

"Get away from there with that thing!" he yelled, a hammer dangling forgotten in his gloved hand.

"Get away from where with what thing?"

"Get away from my greenhouse with that stupid phone!" His tone was sharp and cutting.

I stepped back, stung. Jasher dropped his eyes down to his work, shaking his head and muttering.

Stupid phone? Heat flushed up my neck and across my cheeks. I was paying him a compliment, wasn't I? Showing interest in his work. I thought it beautiful and unique enough to take pictures of, so what was the issue? What right did he have to yell at me?

My vision blurred, and my face felt like it was burning up. I stalked back into the house. My mind whirled and tripped over itself, trying to make sense of him. Maybe he was afraid I'd publish it online and someone would steal his idea or something. Whatever his issue was, he didn't need to be so rude.

I suddenly missed my friends deeply.

I took a shower to scrub the incident from my mind, but it kept creeping back on sharp fingers. I shut off the spray and stepped out of the old clawfoot tub, shivering. I wrapped myself up in a scratchy line-dried towel, turbaned my dripping hair, and closed myself in my room.

I opened my friends' messaging app and attached a photo of the back yard, the one I'd taken from the rear that showed the back of the house, the pond and the gazebo. Targa was the first to respond, and she didn't waste any time getting to the goods.

Targa: *Ok, so the place is amazeballs. We knew that. What about your cuz? What's he like?*

Saxony: *Sí. Give, Georjie.*

In response, I sent the photo I had taken of Jasher. There was a delay in the conversation while the girls took in the photo. I could see them in my mind's eye - zooming in on their phones. Then...

Saxony: 😳 *Is THAT him? This a joke, right?*

Me: *No joke.*

Saxony: *I'm getting on a plane. I'll be right there.*

Targa: *Sheesh! He's no bowl of toads, is he.*

Saxony: *Is he a jerk? He's a jerk, right?*

Me: *He's no picnic.*

Saxony: *Who cares! Look at him!*

Targa: *If you hook up with your cousin...*

Me: *He's not technically my cousin.*

Saxony: *Uh huh. What would your aunt say if you hooked up? *Gasp* Or Liz!*

Me: *He hates me.*

Targa: *?*

Saxony: *Not possible.*

Me: *Possible. He treated me like I strangled his baby panda.*

Saxony: *He's just intimidated. You do that to guys. Even tall ones.*

Me: *No. I'm the intimidated one. I don't know how I'll get through this summer if he doesn't warm up. It's Siberia over here.*

Targa: *Give it some time. He's family.*

Me: *Not technically.*

Saxony: *So you keep saying.*

Me: *But, why does he have to be so pretty?*

Saxony: *Some girls have all the luck.*

Me: *I don't feel lucky. I feel shafted.*

I quickly added:

Me: *Saxony-do not say what you're about to say.*

Saxony: *Mum's the word, darling.*

Targa: *Seriously, just relax. Give it time. You're irresistible.*

Saxony: *Keep us posted on cute mister freeze. This promises to be interesting.*

I put my phone aside. "It sure does," I said.

CHAPTER 6

At first, I was convinced the music was a recording. I had just shoved my empty luggage under the bed and closed my dresser drawers when faint and haunting strains of Spanish guitar reached my ears. Every hair on my forearms stood at attention and I cocked my head, listening. Faith was out working, so it had to be Jasher who'd put the music on.

A moment later, I realized the music was coming from outside. Thinking he must be working while listening to the radio, I went to the window and peered out. There was no one in the yard, and the sawhorses stood lonely by the garage. A small movement in the gazebo caught my eye – a bare foot peeked out, visible from under the gazebo's roof.

Curious, I went downstairs and out into the backyard. I stopped just outside the door. My eyebrows shot up. "Holy…" I breathed. Jasher was *playing* the music. I walked down the stone path very slowly, listening. His back was to me, his body moving with the rhythm of the music. The notes danced around me, rapid and curling, raising gooseflesh. I'd never heard a guitar played with such skill. My heart melted.

He was leaning back on a stool, his back propped against one of the posts. I stopped walking, not sure if I should approach and let him know I was listening, or stand quietly until he was finished and then applaud.

Abruptly, his body stiffened a bit and he stopped playing.

I held my breath. Had he heard me? Was he going to yell at me for something? I was about to tell him how wonderful his playing was when he spoke.

"It's called Asturias," he said.

My mouth dropped open to answer but for some reason, nothing came out. There was something strange in the way he'd spoken, so quietly that it couldn't have been for my benefit.

He spoke again, and the chill that swept my body this time was not from the pleasure of his music. "Isaac Albéniz."

This time, my jaw dropped. He wasn't talking to me, I was certain of it. A moment passed while I stood there frozen, unable to decide what to do.

"I'm not sure exactly," he said, shifting on his stool. He cleared his throat and flapped a hand in the air, indicating an approximation. "Sometime in the eighteen eighties."

I stood rooted to the spot, horrified. The blood must have drained from my head because my vision faded for a moment and then refocused again.

Jasher gave a tight chuckle, like he was forcing himself to relax in the presence of someone he wasn't sure he liked. "Thanks, Conor. If I knew how to do *cante jondo* I would, but my singing voice is diabolical."

My hand flew to my mouth and my eyes stretched open wide. I finally moved, taking a step backward. Who the hell was Conor?

Quiet though it was, my footstep alerted Jasher and he stood up and turned, one hand wrapped around the neck of his guitar. His cold eyes fell on me.

"I'm sorry," I choked out. "I heard you from my room and..."

Jasher's face went pale and then flushed red. His expression grew stormy and he strode past me without a word. The mudroom door clicked shut behind me and I closed my eyes, mortified. I stood there for a long time, not sure what to do, what to think.

Later that night I had processed what had happened enough to send some texts to my friends.

Me: *I think my cousin is crazy.*

Saxony: *Crazy like a fox?*

Targa: *Why do you think that?*

Me: *I caught him speaking to someone who wasn't there.*

Saxony: *I talk to myself all the time. Doesn't make me crazy.*

Me: *Do you address yourself as Stacy?*

Saxony: *Wha?*

Me: *He addressed this invisible person as Conor.*

Targa*: Ho boy.*

Me: *Right?! Helluva guitar player though.*

Saxony: *Like an idiot savant.*

Me: *He's no idiot. You should see the greenhouse he built.* I attached a photo of it and hit send.

Saxony: *Wow! I love a man who's good with his hands.*

Targa: *Does that roof open?!*

Me: *It'll probably do the freaking can-can if you ask it. Jasher is a genius. He hates me, and he's crazy. But he's a genius.*

Targa: *Why don't you just ask him about the... Conor? There must be an explanation.*

Me: *Yeah right! That's how people end up in shallow graves by the roadside.*

Saxony: *Spoken like a true invertebrate.*

CHAPTER 7

After that, Jasher and I avoided each other like the healthy avoided lepers. But we couldn't avoid each other all summer, as much as I would have liked to.

Later that week found me put to work weeding in the garden with Faith. Do I need to tell you how enthusiastic I felt about this particular activity? It was the warmest day since I'd arrived, and there was not a cloud in the sky.

It was mid-afternoon on a Friday and Jasher was home from his latest contract already and working on the greenhouse. He crossed the lawn once in a while to retrieve a window or a tool. I fought not to look up every time I caught him in my periphery. Did Faith know how prickly Jasher was? Or that he might be nuts?

Faith seemed more intent on patiently teaching me how to identify a weed. She didn't trust that I was getting it, though, because she hovered close as the pile of pulled vegetation grew beside me. Smart lady. I yanked at another green thing with roots, which I thought she'd identified as intrusive.

"Not that one, dear. That's Echinacea, great for boosting the immune system."

"Oh, sorry."

"You seem a bit distracted today, Georjie. Everything okay? Not regretting coming to Ireland for the summer, I hope?"

Damn, she was perceptive. "No, Auntie," I lied.

She took her dirty gardening gloves off and wiped her face. "I have to head into town for a late appointment soon, I should get cleaned up. Thirsty? I bought fresh lemons for lemonade."

"Parched." I took my gloves off and followed Faith toward the house. I was wearing an apron and my cell phone was tucked into the front pocket. It chirped with a text. I pulled it out and glanced at the screen.

Saxony: *Have you talked to crazy-pants yet?*

My mouth twitched. Saxony never gave up.

"Have you checked in with your mom?" Faith asked.

I shook my head and dropped my phone back into the pocket. "It's okay. Liz is busy. She won't expect to talk much."

"When did you start calling your mom *Liz*?" Faith asked.

"When she stopped treating me like a daughter," I said, and then clamped my mouth shut. Oops. I was about to apologize when a flying insect buzzed in front of my face. I stepped back and swiped at it. I caught a glimpse of yellow and black stripes. In some shadowy corner of my brain, logic and decorum were shouting not to scream like a nut-case, but they were trapped underneath a huge red boulder labeled *phobia*. The breath was stolen from my lips before I could inhale as memories of intense stinging pain in multiple places all over my body came rushing back.

"Be still, Georjie." Faith's voice echoed around the boulder of phobia. "It won't bother you if you stop trying to kill it."

I froze. Well, sort of. As frozen as you can be while hyperventilating.

"Just be calm, don't move."

Two seconds later, the insect flew away. I hyperventilated for another half-minute before my breathing slowed. I put a hand over my beating heart. That was when the real embarrassment seeped in. But, you have to understand that I didn't know how to behave any differently - this reaction was primal and came from the same place as bad dreams.

Bees and wasps have been my nemesis ever since I was eight. I'd been stung a dozen times while Targa and I were playing in the woods near my house. Liz lost her mind and took me screaming to the hospital - by which I mean she was the one screaming - solidifying in my young mind that anything with stripes and stinger was the devil incarnate. I learned later why she'd lost her mind. She didn't know if I was allergic. I wasn't, thank goodness. But I had been left with a different sort of damage - the kind that scars your psyche.

"Good heavens, Georjayna," Faith said, putting a warm hand on my arm. "I thought you were joking about the bee thing. You weren't afraid of insects last time you were here. What happened?"

Jasher's head poked round the side of the greenhouse. He disappeared again and I was sure that I heard stifled laughter. Was I imagining it? My face flushed. "Got stung by a bee… bees, multiple," I said, mortified. A bright bitter hate welled up for the tiny creature that had caused me to humiliate myself, as acidic as lemon juice.

Faith did what people who didn't have any phobias did - tried to rationalize my fear away. "We love bees. You know that without them the human race would perish? Seventy percent of the world's food supply is pollinated by bees."

"Yes, Auntie. I do know that. Logically." And I did. There had been a 'Save the Bees' campaign at school last year because some mysterious force was killing bees all over the world. I had read the material. I knew that the little black and yellow demons were a necessary evil. That didn't help during close encounters of the stinging kind.

"Anyway, that wasn't a bee you saw," she said. "It was a hornet. Jasher!" Faith called, startling me.

Please no. Hadn't I had enough embarrassment for one day? To my horror, Jasher came striding across the grass towards us, looking gorgeous and amused. Oh, how I hated him in that moment.

"Yeah?"

I wanted to slap the smirk off his face. He might be crazy but he obviously didn't have any phobias, at least, that's what I thought at the time. If I had known then what I know now, I would have had a lot more grace about the whole thing. As it was, I wanted to stick my tongue out at him. Or just haul off and round-house him. I've got long legs. I could have reached his head.

"Would you like to teach your cousin the fascinating art of search and destroy?"

Search and destroy? I blinked at my nature-loving aunt. Just when you think you know someone...

Jasher didn't answer at first. Then, "If I were mad."

My jaw dropped and I stared at him.

"Jasher," said Faith, reproachfully.

"She's plankin' it. You want me to hunt for the nest with *her* in tow?" He hadn't even looked at me.

A red-hot jolt of anger made my heart pound and my face flush. I was the subject of the conversation and he was treating me like I wasn't even there.

"No, I'd like to see this trick of yours, *Jasher*," I replied.

He finally looked me in the eye. He must have seen the challenge there. "Have it your way."

He headed for the house. I followed him, mutely hoping I wasn't going to regret my bravado. He went into the kitchen, opened the refrigerator, and pulled out a package of stewing beef. He opened the package and took out a piece of the meat. Once the package was returned to the fridge, he headed back outside, holding the piece of beef.

Bemused, I followed him to the garage where he rummaged around on the cluttered shelves. He grabbed a long pole with a hook on the end of it. Next he took a tackle box from a bottom shelf, and plopped it on an oil-stained table. He opened the lid and retrieved some fishing line and a small white feather. So far, Jasher hadn't said a word or acknowledged me in any way. He left the garage with his hornet destroying gear and I followed, feeling like an idiot.

Faith watched us as Jasher strode across the enormous lawn toward the trees at the rear of the property. I trailed after him like a lost puppy.

Just inside the forest, Jasher stopped. He hooked the piece of beef on the end of the pole and then handed it to me. "Hold this," he ordered. "And keep it still."

I watched, fascinated in spite of myself, as his dexterous hands formed a loop with the filament. Then he attached the white feather to the tiny lasso he'd created. I wished he'd give me some running commentary about what he was doing, but I wasn't about to give him the satisfaction of asking. Then he sat down at the trunk of a tree, leaving me standing there with the pole. I had never felt so stupid in my life. I finally sat down beside him and we waited in silence, me holding the pole with the chunk of beef on the end of it, and him leaning against the tree with his head tilted back.

After nearly ten minutes of this nonsense it was on the tip of my tongue to ask him what the hell we were doing, when two small colored things zipped by in my periphery. I snapped my head to the side to get a better look, but couldn't see anything.

"Did you see that?" I asked.

"What?" Jasher said. His face had a smug look, like he knew something I didn't.

I gritted my teeth. I was about to call him cocky, or arrogant, or something suitably stinging when he held his hand out for the pole. His gaze was directed upward at the beef.

"Hand it over slow," he said.

I looked up and gulped. A hornet buzzed around the beef. My insides quivered. I moved the pole over to his hand and he took it, his fingers brushing mine. Keeping the butt end of the pole propped against the ground, he got to his feet. I did the same, anticipating an attack to the head. I stepped away from the pole. To my horror, Jasher slid the pole through his hands, drawing the hornet toward himself. My breathing hitched and his eyes flashed to my face. He was waiting for me to flip out. I steeled myself, fists clenched.

The hornet was closer now, and my whole body was vibrating. Fear clutched at my belly. It was sheer stubbornness that kept me from bolting away like my hair was on fire. I could not have drawn my eyes away from the vile thing even if I had wanted to. The hornet munched on the beef happily, its disgusting little mandibles gouging into the flesh. It paid us no mind. Its striped abdomen pulsed, making it look like that's where its heart was.

Holding the pole steady, Jasher lifted the tiny filament lasso towards the hornet. I held my breath and watched, fascinated and repulsed. He slipped the loop over its abdomen and tightened it around its tiny waist. He took his hand away and my jaw went slack. The hornet was still eating, oblivious. The white feather was now suspended from its body. By then, my amazement surpassed my terror.

"You're still here," Jasher said, under his breath.

"I guess crazy comes in contagious," I replied through a tight jaw.

He huffed a surprised laugh and the hornet buzzed its wings. I had never felt such a deep satisfaction at anyone's laugh in my life before. If I hadn't been so afraid, I would have allowed myself to smile.

"You haven't seen crazy yet," he said.

I was about to mutter, 'Are you sure about that?' when the hornet took off, carrying the feather with it. Jasher took off after it, and I took off after Jasher.

We pelted full-tilt through the woods as the white feather zigzagged through the air, seemingly of its own accord. The feather rose and our necks craned to follow. I stumbled as my foot rolled over a rotting branch. I recovered and kept running. It was all I could do to keep up with Jasher. Sunlight flashed into my eyes through the canopy and my hands hooked on trees as we darted past them on a serpentine course through the woods. My heart and breath worked on overdrive. Our footfalls were almost completely muffled by the thick ground cover of leaves, needles, and dirt. The feather bobbed and weaved through the woods. I lost it several times, but Jasher never did. Clearly, he'd done this before.

Just when I thought I couldn't go any further, Jasher pulled up short. I skidded but couldn't stop in time and crashed into the back of him.

"Oooof!" Air whooshed out of me.

He didn't budge. I may as well have hit a tree. His broad back was solid and unforgiving. He put his arms behind himself in a reflex to catch me and his hands found my hips. His fingers curled around my hip bones. The touch was sudden and intimate and my heart tripped on its wheel. He let go quickly.

"Sorry," I gasped, stepping back and bending over to catch my breath. I was sucking air hard, but he was hardly huffing. I looked up at him when he didn't reply.

His gaze was fixed above us. I stood and craned my neck, putting a palm to my thudding heart. Up in the tree was a large gray nest. Hundreds of hornets buzzed around it. Both of my hands clamped over my mouth to cut off my scream. I inhaled sharply through my nose and Jasher glanced at me. I'm sure I looked like I was about to vomit.

The hornets had built their nest under a branch. It looked like it had been shoved into the tree's armpit. The white feather buzzed around the nest. The visual was bizarre.

In the battle of phobia over pride, phobia finally won. I took several steps back. I took my hands away from my mouth when I was sure I wasn't going to scream.

"Congratulations," I said between deep breaths. "Can I go now?"

He jerked his chin toward the house in a dismissive gesture. "Go," he said. He rummaged in his pocket, producing a lighter and a pocket knife.

I backed away, stung again by his cold tone. I wasn't sure if a bee-sting would have been worse. I turned and started back to towards the house.

There was a muffled sound behind me. "Ynnngh knwww..."

I turned back.

He had one glove clamped between his perfect teeth and was pulling the other one onto his hand. He took the glove out of his mouth. "You know how to get back?"

"Yes," I said. What did he care?

He nodded and turned back to his work.

I turned away again.

"Georjayna." It was the first time I'd heard my name on his lips. I hated how much I loved the way it sounded. He looked me in the eyes for the second time that day. Was that a modicum of respect I saw? "Fair play to ye."

A warm, liquid sensation pooled in my limbs. The feeling mingled with a deep annoyance at the pleasure those three words gave me, just because they'd come from him. How stupid. I'd never craved approval from a man before, and certainly not one who appeared to have mental health issues. It was the kind of thing I had judged Saxony for. I nodded and turned away.

I walked until my heart calmed, and then began to jog again. My limbs felt antsy and full of adrenalin. When I was a safe distance from the hornets' nest, the realization of what had happened began to sink in. I shook my head in amazement. What kind of person knew how to lasso a hornet and then follow it to its nest? Curiosity burbled in me like a fountain. I looked forward to being alone with Faith so I could pepper her with questions. But by the time I got back to the house, Faith had already left for the day.

CHAPTER 8

The next morning, I found Aunt Faith in the kitchen wearing an apron and peering at a book laid open on the island counter. Reading glasses were perched on the end of her nose and for a second, she reminded me of Liz.

She peered over the rims at me. "Morning. Sleep well?"

"Yes, thanks," I mumbled, shuffling to the fridge in my slippers and filling a glass with water from the filter in the door.

"How did the search and destroy exercise go? You guys were both in bed by the time I got home." Faith opened the oven and pulled out a tray of hot scones. "I thought I might have a real teenager to deal with this summer. You know, coming home at three in the morning from parties and such." Faith said, fanning the steaming scones and inhaling the scented steam. "Turns out I've got two geriatrics on my hands instead."

I smiled. More like two mutes. The evening before, Jasher and I looked after our own meals and barely spent a minute in the same room together.

"I've never been a big one for parties where I don't know anyone," I said. "Although an Irish dust-up might be fun."

“The local kids have a party every summer at the old Eithne place. You could ask Jasher to take you.”

“Fat chance of that,” I muttered, as she closed the oven door with a snap.

She turned to me, taking off her oven mitts. “What was that, dear?

“Nothing.” I perched on the stool at the island, my mouth watering at the smell of fresh baking. "In the war of man versus hornet yesterday, man won by a landslide.”

"Yes, they really don’t have a chance against him.” She produced a colander full of tomatoes from the sink and placed them on a towel on the island. “Want to help me? Jasher will be popping in for breakfast at half-eight."

"You mean second breakfast?" I said.

Faith laughed. Jasher was up and working by five-thirty every morning except for Sundays. His schedule would make me cry.

“Would you like to slice these in half?" she asked, pushing the tomatoes across the counter toward me. She bent and produced a serrated knife from the drawer. “Jasher likes them broiled.”

"Of course." I grabbed a cutting board from a peg on the wall and got to work. "So, where did he learn that trick?"

"Lassoing a hornet? Believe it or not, he already knew how to do that before he came to me."

"Really?" I was surprised. "But he was pretty young. Did he tell you where he learned it?"

"Not right away. The first time I saw him do it, he was only nine. I never would have believed it if I hadn't seen it with my own eyes. He told me he *just knew* how to do it. But he had to have learned it somewhere. Kids aren't born knowing things like that. He was just afraid to tell me.” Faith laid a baking sheet out beside me.

"Did he eventually tell you?" I put the tomatoes cut side up on the pan.

"Not plainly, no. I had to figure it out for myself."

"How did you manage that?"

"To explain how I figured it out, I'd have to go back to the beginning." Faith took a pair of scissors from a drawer and went to the window. She snipped off several stems from one of the plants. She held it up to my nose. "Smell that."

A pungent smell filled my nostrils. "Eurgh." My eyes watered.

"Nothing beats fresh oregano and tomatoes," she said with a smile.

"I'll take your word for it," I said, wanting to get back to Jasher. "I don't know about you, but I have all day. He won't mind you telling me the story, I'm family," I said, thinking that I felt the very opposite of Jasher's family. Around him, I felt like an outsider.

"Yes, I know you are, dear," Faith said. "It's just, well it's very personal and a bit disquieting, if you get my meaning."

I didn't, but I nodded.

She took a deep breath. "Where to start. His mother, Maud, died in childbirth, poor woman." Faith drizzled olive oil over the tomatoes and snipped oregano so it dusted each one. The strong scent filled the kitchen.

"Yes, I read about her in your letters. What happened to her?"

"She hemorrhaged and died from loss of blood, which is tragic all by itself. The really strange thing is that she died *before* she had a chance to birth Jasher. We should have lost the wee lad too, but..." She paused. "Well, I have never seen anything like it."

"What do you mean?" The faraway expression on her face was giving me chills.

Faith put the tray of tomatoes under the broiler and shut the oven. She turned to me. "If a pregnant woman dies, the infant dies, too. Sometimes they can be rescued through cesarean, but it happened so quickly and we were so focused on trying to stop the bleeding that it caught us unaware. It was a matter of moments from the time she started hemorrhaging until she was clinically deceased - no breath, no heartbeat. But incredibly, as we were trying to change course to save the babe, Maud's body continued to birth the child." I saw a tremor pass through her. "We all knew we were witnessing a miracle. Her body continued to push for another half hour. We didn't know what to do, since the poor wee thing was already in the birth canal by the time we got ourselves turned around. It was incredible, horrifying, and impossible, all at the same time."

We both fell silent. Goosebumps crawled up the back of my neck and over my scalp. I imagined seeing the corpse of a pregnant woman, the body straining actively with the climax of birth contractions, the eyes dead and unseeing. A round of nausea made my mouth water.

"That was a good mam, I'll tell you that," Faith said. "She loved that child from beyond the grave."

"But, how is it possible?" I took a glass from the cupboard and poured some water. "Did you ask around and see if that kind of thing had ever happened before?" I took a few big gulps and my stomach gurgled in response. I put a hand to my belly, not quite sure if I had done it a favor or not.

"Oh yes," Faith said. "We were all confounded. The hospital administrator went straight to his rolodex, asking for reports of other cases. Not a one came back. I sent a letter to one of my old friends from University, a man who attended literally hundreds of births. He'd never heard of such a thing and bade me to let it rest. Jasher's father was none too pleased with the attention it brought. There were countless requests for interviews and studies. He was against all of it. Can't say I blamed the man."

"What happened to Jasher's father?" I asked, glancing out the window into the back yard. No sign of Jasher yet.

"That's also a sad story," Faith said. "At first he seemed okay. He had to grieve of course but he took Jasher home and tried to raise him alone. What else could he do? Unfortunately for Jasher, his father came to blame his son for his wife's death. He abused the boy something terrible I'm afraid." She joined me at the back window, her gray eyes finding the horizon. "His da remembered me from the birth and he came to me a few times to ask me to take Jasher. He had no other family, and very few friends by this point. He said the boy was cursed, a child of the devil and all that nonsense."

I gasped. "What did you say?"

"I tried to talk some sense into him and when I couldn't, I encouraged him to seek council. Then, one summer, I was weeding in the garden when I heard the sound of a vehicle stop at the end of the driveway. A door opened and closed and then the car continued on.

Jasher came wandering into the yard all by himself. I'll always remember how he looked that day. Both of his little skinny arms were covered in bruises and he had a black eye. He was carrying a duffle that had everything in it that he owned in the world. He said that his da told him I'd look after him."

I visualized the scene, my heart aching for that kid. "What did you do?"

"I told him that of course I would look after him. I gave him a hug and he let me hold him on my lap on the porch for an hour. I became a mother that day." She too watched the yard for a sign of her adopted son. "To this day I am so glad that I didn't stop to think about it. The poor wee thing had been rejected and beaten by his own father, blamed for his mother's death, and then told I was the only person in the world who would accept him. If I had showed him a moment's hesitation, he would never believe that I really loved him." She moved to the table and sat down. "My life had not been heading in the direction of motherhood. But sometimes, it seems like there are other plans in motion for our lives, whether we like it or not."

I thought about how I had not been planning to come to Ireland, but through circumstances that were out of my control, here I was.

Faith stared down at her hands and chewed her lip. A line had formed between her brows.

"That's only half of it." She took a breath. "Going back to the lassoing of hornets. When I asked him where he learned it, at first he wouldn't say. When I kept asking him, he said that an old Chinese man had showed him. He wouldn't say who the man was or where he'd met him. I couldn't make sense of it. I wracked my brains to think of a Chinese man in Ana that Jasher could have met but couldn't think of a single one. I prodded him for almost a year before I figured it out."

I sank into the chair across from her, my heart thudding. The nameless sensation shrouded me, the back of my neck prickled.

"I uncovered more clues and eventually I had enough to piece things together. I'm not sure it would have happened if it wasn't for Sarasborne. This place has been renovated and added to over the years, but it still has the same foundation and most of the original building is intact. It has its tragedies, too."

Tragedies? I wracked my brains for anything Liz might have told me and came up empty.

Faith poured herself a glass of water and took a sip. "My Grandfather Syracuse used to tell stories to your mam and me. One of them was about a young man who had been killed during the construction of this place. Sarasborne was nearly finished and the men were doing the roof. The pitch is steep and the men had to rig up scaffolding and ropes and the like for safety. One of the men, Conor, slipped and fell. He was roped, but in those days there was no such thing as nylon and the rope had no give. He was saved from hitting the ground, but the internal injuries killed him."

Conor. I grew very still. My mouth had gone dry. "This place has a ghost?"

Faith nodded and went on. "Neither your mam nor I ever saw anything strange, and believe you me, we looked. As kids we were obsessed. We'd half convinced ourselves that objects had been moved from room to room or that doors had opened on their own. But if I'm really honest I know that we never witnessed anything of real proof. But, about a year after the first time I watched Jasher put a feather on a hornet - it was late one night when I heard his voice. I thought he was talking in his sleep so I stopped outside his room to listen. I realized a conversation was going on." Faith stared past me with unseeing eyes. "I peeked into his room. It was a full moon so the room was bright. He was sitting up in bed with his back against a pillow, relaxed as you please and havin' a gas with someone I couldn't see."

My skin had turned clammy, in spite of the warmth of the room. It was just like the conversation I'd witnessed while Jasher was playing the guitar. I could imagine how Faith would have felt that night.

"I was frightened," she was saying. "Then I caught the drift of the conversation. Someone was explaining to Jasher how this house had been built. He asked the man's name, waited for a moment and then said, "It's nice to meet you Conor, I'm Jasher."

I shook my head. "You'd never told him about Conor."

"No, never. He was too young to be hearin' stories like that. So that's when I knew that the boy I'd adopted could speak to the dead."

I was shaken, because I knew she was telling the truth.

"After that, I took my time," she continued. "Eventually, I asked Jasher if the old Chinese man who had taught him how to lasso hornets had been a ghost, and he said 'yes'." Her eyes misted over and her voice broke. "Then he looked so guilty and I told him that he didn't ever need to be ashamed. After that he seemed relieved that he didn't have to hide it from me anymore."

I absorbed everything she'd told me. While sitting around a campfire and telling ghost stories plays a part in every child's life, I always knew they were just stories. But this wasn't just a story, it had happened here, in this house, to my family.

"There are those who say that Ana County is situated on a ley line, and that's why supernatural things happen here more often than other places."

"Ley line?" I'd never heard the term before.

"An undetectable matrix of energy lines criss-crossing the earth. Some say they link sites of supernatural significance such as the pyramids and Stonehenge, just to name two obvious ones. Others say that the lines were there before things like that were built, and because the lines are so rich with electromagnetic power, they attract supernatural activity."

"Whoa. Auntie," I gave her a spooked side-eye and she laughed.

"I know." She opened the oven and the smell of broiled tomatoes filled the kitchen. "To someone who doesn't work with energy on a regular basis, it sounds kooky. But I can assure you it only seems flaky to those whose worldview is rooted in the tangible world. No one can deny that there's power in the earth - how else would plants grow or volcanoes explode? She shrugged and put the tray of tomatoes on the island to cool. "It's not so farfetched."

The lens of my own worldview was being challenged just by learning about Jasher's birth and ability. One thing at a time or I would feel overwhelmed. "Do you think Jasher sees ghosts all the time?"

"I don't know anymore," she said. "I think he used to, when he would go into town for school. I couldn't figure out why he was so thin and anxious all the time. But after I took him out and home-schooled him for a while, he was a completely different boy."

"How so?" I peered out the window, keeping watch for the man himself. I felt a little guilty that we were talking about Jasher in such detail while he wasn't there. By now I knew way more about him than he knew about me. Advantage Georjayna. So I guess I didn't feel *that* guilty.

Faith laughed, took off her glasses, and wiped her eyes. "Sometimes children really do know best. Homeschooling was his idea. I was against keeping him at home permanently at first; I just wanted him to do it for a year to get his health back. I wanted him to have friends his age and to receive the same privileges that other children had. But when the time came to register him in school again, he begged me not to make him go back. He was so desperate not to that I hired tutors and he surprised both of us by graduating early. He always had terrible grades at public school. But without all the... distractions... of whatever he was dealing with in town, he was a star. Not long after he graduated, he started the landscaping business and he seems to be okay doing that for now. He doesn't mention the dead anymore."

Movement through the window caught my eye. Jasher was striding across the lawn toward the house. He looked completely different to me now that I knew more of his story. He walked with a confidence rarely seen in those who'd suffered so much at a young age. There were troubled kids in my high school, and they weren't hard to spot. It was in the fearful eyes and the posture that said *don't look at me.* Jasher displayed neither.

"Do you think," I asked as we watched him approach, "that the circumstances of his birth have anything to do with his ability to talk to the dead?"

Faith smiled and waved at Jasher through the glass. He waved back and gave us a heart-stopping grin. His white teeth flashed in his tanned face, changing his entire countenance. I found myself wishing the grin was for me, but I knew that it was for Faith. I understood their bond now.

Faith said, "I have wondered that myself countless times. He didn't just get too close to the veil, he was inside it. That kind of beginning is bound to leave its mark."

The door to the mudroom opened and Faith went to the cupboard for plates.

CHAPTER 9

Second breakfast was quick and quiet. I didn't feel much like making conversation after what Faith had told me. My mental processor was already working overtime. Jasher wasn't talkative at the best of times, and Faith barely said a word either. We each seemed lost in our own wells of personal thought. We ate breakfast in the gazebo while birds chirped and butterflies fluttered through the garden.

Jasher had barely swallowed his last bite when he kissed Faith on the cheek and dismissed himself, claiming he needed to run errands. He gave me a curt nod goodbye and I considered it an improvement. Once Jasher had gone, the atmosphere eased.

"What's Jasher doing to the greenhouse?" I asked Faith as we did the dishes together. "I saw there's a window that needs fixing, but he's got a lot more windows there than he needs to do that job."

"He's expanding it," she explained. "I'm not sure where he gets his ideas from but once he's got a plan in his head, there isn't any stopping him." She looked me in the eye as she wiped down the counter top. "One of the reasons I'm so glad you've come for the summer is because I think it will be good for him to spend some time with someone his own age. I don't want to force him to go out into the world if that's not what he wants, but I don't want him to be sheltered forever, either." She put a hand on my upper arm and squeezed it. "Thanks for coming, Georjayna."

I flushed. "Thanks for having me." What else could I say? I had been under the impression that Aunt Faith took me in as a favor to Liz, but apparently that's not the way Faith saw it.

"Have you seen the greenhouse yet?" Faith asked.

"Just from the outside." It was on the tip of my tongue to ask Faith about Jasher's prickliness, but I didn't have the courage to bring it up. Faith was leaving for Aberdeen in a week, and so far Jasher and I were getting along like two wounded badgers stuck in a pipe, but I didn't want to tattle. I can't bear the sound of whining, especially my own. No, if Jasher had a problem with me, I was going to have to deal with it myself.

Faith gestured for me to follow her. We left the kitchen and went down the long dark hallway that ran through the center of the house. The parlor was an L-shaped sitting room complete with a fireplace, overstuffed chairs, and cracked paintings of rolling green landscapes.

The room was dim, so I reached for the light switch.

"There's no power to this side of the house," said Faith.

I dropped my hand. "Oh, it went out?"

"Sort of." Faith smoothly slid the handmade glass doors wide. Richly scented, humid air drifted in through the open door. I followed her into the jungle. A long narrow walkway, the neck of the key, opened up into the round room under the dome. I hadn't spent much time in hothouses in my life, but even I knew this was no ordinary greenhouse. Humans were not in charge here - plants were. Little hand-made signs populated the entire greenhouse. I still couldn't tell what was what. Everything criss-crossed in a thick tangle of green.

The floor of the greenhouse was naked earth and many of the plants grew directly from the ground. Others flourished in terra cotta pots and strawberry planters. A few plants thrived in raised beds retained by low wooden walls. Wrought iron structures supported climbing vines. The structures themselves were nearly obscured as they'd been covered in leaves.

"Did Jasher make these, too?" I asked, gesturing to the shapes.

"Yes. Lovely, aren't they?"

I nodded, admiring the curving, feminine shapes. I was having trouble reconciling Jasher with these pretty works of art. Was there anything he didn't know how to make?

Faith pointed out some of the more powerful medicinal plants, since these were the reason she'd wanted a greenhouse in the first place. She had a small worktable and shelving that was bursting with amber glass bottles, each one hand-labeled in a delicate script.

She explained that Jasher would be building a bigger workshop for her as part of the expansion. She'd been able to foster relationships with a few boutique stores and had small orders to fill for essential oils. A small distillery sat on a low long table beside her cupboards.

The sound of wings made me look up. "There's a bird in here!" I exclaimed, tracking a sparrow flitting from one branch to another, tilting its head at us. "How can we help it get outside?"

Faith was unconcerned. "Do you see the seams in the dome that run through the center in the shape of a cross?" My eye followed where she pointed.

"Yes." I could see them, and a pulley system attached to a spool and handle that was at waist height and hidden in the foliage. Targa had been right after all. "The dome opens?"

"Yes. Watch." Faith moved the leaves aside and began to crank the handle. The ceiling of the dome opened outward like a flower opening up to the sun. The petals came to rest, folded entirely backward on themselves. The swallow vanished through the open dome.

I was genuinely impressed. I knew nothing about architecture or mechanical things. Jasher seemed more and more like a magician to me. Too bad he was such a grump. "I guess in the summer, there isn't much need to shelter all these plants."

"Exactly. It can get too hot so we keep it open most of the time. Pure rainwater is mother's milk for plants, and keeping the roof open also allows pollinators like bees to come in. Don't worry, they don't stay," she said quickly when she saw the look on my face. "They just come and do their job and then go home." She began to close the dome again, turning the crank.

"You're not going to leave it open?" I watched the big glass flower close into a bud.

"Not for tonight," she said. "The forecast calls for a pretty strong overnight electrical storm. I don't want to wake up to a swamp in here."

I trailed after Faith as she sealed up the greenhouse, not wanting to leave. I couldn't put my finger on what it was, but the place had a kind of magnetism that made me want to stay.

CHAPTER 10

Now that I'm looking back on everything in retrospect, the first dream comes to me as clear as water from a spring-fed stream. I know now that it was really more of a vision, and it happened sometime during the darkest part of the night.

I remember floating on air. I don't remember where exactly I was, but I remember my legs moving as though walking but the soles of my feet made no contact with anything solid. An ethereal fog blew around me as I pedaled against nothing. The soft cotton cloth of my pajamas brushed against my legs. My legs continued to stroll, my hair blew gently, tendrils kissing my cheeks. I remember feeling quite strongly that there was something that urgently needed my attention. Me. Georjayna Sutherland. Only I would do.

A bookcase with glass doors materialized in the gloom and I pedaled toward it. Grasping the cupboard handles, I opened both doors wide. The faint scent of old leather drifted out. I trailed a fingertip across the spines of the unusually tall leather-bound books. None of them were embossed or printed with a title.

The same feeling that told me something needed my attention also told me which book to choose. I hooked my finger into the top of a frayed looking spine and pulled. It slid out and fell open in my hands.

The spine cracked. On the oversized page was a painting rendered in colored ink, as beautiful and vivid as a stained-glass window. An elaborate border in multi-colored paisley and gold leaf framed the portrait. The subject's tiny face was all spritely angles. Slashes of dark hair fell across her ears and shoulders. Wispy, fine wings rose elegantly from her back. The delicate fingers of her right hand reached out, seeming to rise from the page. A name sounded off in my mind, like the tinkling of a very far away bell. I heard a wind, and words on the wind.

Say her name.

"Eda," I whispered. The smell of moss and damp earth filled my senses. The warm night breeze blew my hair away from my face and off my shoulders. Grass touched the tips of my toes as they hung above the earth and I remember not thinking it was odd at all that this bookcase was outside. I turned the page.

Another exquisite painting. This portrait was of a masculine faerie, with squared-off wings and strong looking legs. I knew his name, too. It appeared in my mind like a thought that had been delivered. It's weird what our minds do in the nighttime. The wind that spoke repeated itself.

Say his name.

"'Po," I said, louder this time. The warm breeze caressed my cheek bones, caught at my eyelashes. My toes touched the earth as I dropped another fraction. I turned the page again.

Another sketch. Another name. Another whisper. Another breath. Each time, more of my soles made contact with the soil and grass beneath my feet.

"Tera. Hana. J'al. Mehda."

I turned the pages faster, feeling compelled to say every name out loud. With every name, the warm wind grew stronger, whipping my hair around. The fabric of my pajamas lay completely still despite the gale. There was a long drawn out 'haaaaaaaaaaaa', sound - like an exhale, warm and humid. I went on, naming names.

"Oka. Iri. Bolé. Wenn."

I inhaled the warm earthy wind, and it filled my lungs, energized me. My weight settled fully onto the soles of my feet.

It was enough. I was finished. My job was done, for now.

I replaced the book and closed the glass doors with a click as the swirling fog closed in around me.

CHAPTER 11

It was the booming sound of distant thunder that woke me. I lifted my head to find the clock on my nightstand but it was so dark I couldn't read the face of it as it was an old-fashioned clock, not a digital one. A flash of lightening conveniently lit my room and revealed that it was 5:45. The darkness enveloped me again.

I knew that I'd dreamt something strange, something about wind, and the bottoms of my feet, and the smell of earth after a rain, but I couldn't bring to memory any distinct details. I closed my eyes and wracked my brain but it was hazy at best and just left me with a feeling of confused wonder.

I threw back the covers as rain began to fall in earnest. It pounded the roof and eaves. I've always loved storms. I love when heavy raindrops fall against the windows and run down in sheets against the glass, making the outside world look like it's underwater. I love the rumble of thunder and the white flashes that light up the sky and clouds with painful clarity.

I looked down into the yard but I couldn't make out much through the blur of water except for the dark shape of the gazebo. I wrapped my robe around me and went downstairs to the kitchen to get a better view. The house was quiet. I assumed Jasher and Faith were still sleeping.

The kitchen was lit up by a flash of lightning just as I entered and I was treated to a stark view of the backyard - the dripping wisteria on the terrace, the patio furniture.

I thought the greenhouse would be a good place to enjoy the surround sound experience of rain pelting glass, and lightning illuminating the plants.

The greenhouse sliding door was already open and there was some small source of light - I could see the blurry glow through the panes. I poked my head in. The dome was closed against the driving rain and Jasher sat cross-legged on a mat directly underneath it on the floor, stooped over something in his lap. A long-necked lamp sat on the floor nearby and fed light on whatever he was doing. I turned to leave him to his private time but then stopped. Now was as good a time as any to make another attempt at friendship, even a tentative one.

"Good morning. I guess you had a similar idea. Do you like storms, too?" I padded over the rubber mats on the earthen floor in my slippers. My nerves twanged, the way they always did around Jasher. At the sound of my voice, Jasher snapped a book shut and looked up at me. Was he embarrassed?

"I do like storms." His eyes narrowed. "Please tell me you didn't bring your cell phone in here?" He eyeballed the pocket of my bathrobe.

"After the tongue lashing you gave me?" I replied coolly. "I know better than that, although I have to admit I still don't get it."

He had the decency to look sheepish but the look was gone as quickly as it had come. He propped the book against his chest, like he wanted to hide the title. There was an awkward silence. I hate awkward silences, but I wanted to see if he'd fill it, so I waited. He waited, too. Clearly, he had no intention of sharing with me whatever it was he was reading. I fought the urge to roll my eyes in annoyance. This kind of behavior suited twelve-year-olds.

I was about to turn and leave when he said, "Did you sleep well?"

"Like the dead," I murmured. The dream had vanished completely by then. "You?"

He shrugged. The silence grew heavy and I opened my mouth to dismiss myself for a third time when he said, "Did Faith show you the butterfly cocoons yet?"

I cocked my head. "No. You have butterflies in here somewhere?"

"We do," he said with more enthusiasm than really seemed necessary. I felt thankful that he was making an effort, disingenuous though it was.

"They're over here." Jasher got to his feet and tucked the book underneath his arm. He crouched in front of a thick wall of vines and parted them, revealing several cocoons hanging from the undersides of the leaves. No wonder I hadn't spotted them before; they were completely camouflaged.

"Here." He pointed to several cocoons lined along the same stem. There were nearly a dozen of them. "These ones are Monarchs, and these little guys are called Skippers." He pointed to a couple of smaller, gray ones. His fingertip moved to point out the various species, naming them all. "A Red Admiral, a Peacock, a Tortoise-Shell, a Marbled White, a Meadow Brown and two Gatekeepers. Most of those are from the Nymphalidae family. These ones are Holly Blues, they'll be an amazing periwinkle color. They're from the Lycaenidae family. They all have Latin names of course, but I won't bore you with those."

"It's anything but boring." I wanted to point out that I'd never heard him string so many words together all at once, but he was on a roll now. I didn't want to discourage him by making a joke about it. "How did you get them here, all in the same place?"

"It's not difficult," he said. "I find them in the garden when they're close to making a cocoon and I bring them in here and place them where I know they'll like it." He looked at them with affection. "Sometimes they wander a bit, but most times they build their cocoons right here."

I pointed to a bright purple cocoon shaped exactly like a droplet of water and just as small. It was pearly and exquisite. Odd that he hadn't pointed it out to me yet. "What kind is this one? It's gorgeous."

When he didn't answer, I looked at his face. I'll never forget that look. He was staring at me, spectral eyes in the gloom. Even in the dim light, his shock was the most genuine expression I'd seen on his face since we'd met.

"You can see that one?" He pointed. "This purple one, right here?"

"Yes, of course. Why shouldn't I see it?"

His normally ruddy face took on a waxy cast.

"Jasher, are you okay?" I put a hand on his shoulder. It was the first time I'd touched him intentionally since our spiky handshake. The corded muscle under my palm jumped.

"Have you ever seen a cocoon like this one before?" he asked.

"No, I'm sure I haven't. Why? Is it rare?"

"Never? Never, ever?" He emphasized by slicing his hand through the air - sharp, knife-like. It was really important to him to know that this was the first time.

"Never." I shook my head. I was certain I hadn't. It still didn't explain why he had the complexion of a vampire. "What's the big deal?"

He looked me square in the eyes and said without a hint of a joke, "It's a faerie cocoon."

CHAPTER 12

The rain pelting against the glass became a hail of bullets in the silence. Jasher's dark eyes bored into mine and I couldn't look away. Was he messing with me? I didn't know him well enough to tell. He looked as serious as death. I pressed my lips between my teeth and narrowed my eyes. Several heartbeats pounded past and neither of us spoke.

I released my lips with a little popping sound. "Excuse me?" An uncertain anger bubbled under the surface, wondering if it was justified in showing its head or not. I suspected that he was trying to make me feel foolish. I had no reason to trust him.

"What you're seeing, and trust me, I'm more gobsmacked about it than you are," Jasher said, "is a brand new faerie. This is how they start."

I had the strangest feeling that I should be insulted. It was that moment right then, that I liked him least of all, even less than when he'd snapped at me. The feeling that I couldn't trust him muddied everything, like too much salt can ruin a dish.

"Right." I stood and turned away. Ghosts I could wrap my head around. Faeries? Nope.

His hand caught mine and held it. The warmth of it startled me, but not as much as the tone of his voice when he said, "I'm not lying to you, Georjie. Please don't go."

I paused, and searched his face for dishonesty. I found none, but I still didn't trust him.

"I've never met anyone else who can see them," he went on, his voice soft. "Even Faith, she knows I can see them and believes me, but she can't see them herself. You'll believe me when you see it hatch."

"If you're messing with me..." My voice loaded with threat is still a bit lame, but I did my best.

"I'm not. I wouldn't do that." His accent had grown thicker, which was even more convincing than his words at showing me he was sincere. That, and the energy between us had completely changed. It felt like Jasher had been tolerating me before, but now it felt like he needed an ally, and that ally was me. The switch was so abrupt it gave me vertigo.

I crouched hesitantly and examined the cocoon again. I pushed aside the leaves until what little light there was illuminated it. It certainly didn't look like anything I'd ever seen before, and it didn't look plastic. It was a million shades of swirling pearlescent purple.

Jasher knelt beside me. "You're sure you've never seen one like this before?"

"Jasher, you've asked me that four thousand times. No, I promise I haven't."

"So, why now?" he murmured, more to himself.

"Was there a... a caterpillar?" I felt stupid just asking. "A faerie worm?" I almost giggled at the idea.

"No, that's what's so amazing!" Jasher's voice came out loaded with passion and it caught me up. His eyes were lit and he stared at the cocoon with real affection. "It's the result of dappled sunlight and pure rainwater. I used to find them more often but they're forming less and less, now. They seem to only happen under the right conditions. Like, after a rainstorm when the raindrops are falling more slowly and the sun comes out. I don't know exactly what happens, scientifically speaking, but see how the cocoon looks like a water droplet just about to fall?"

"Mmmmhmmmmm." I noticed a subtle shift in myself. I *wanted* to believe.

"Right at that moment, before it lets go of the leaf, the droplet is penetrated by a beam of sunlight. It doesn't happen in steady, streaming light, only when there are either moving clouds, or tree branches waving around. I reckon it cuts the sunbeams up." He was animated now, like a mad scientist in theorizing mode. "I don't know if the temperature of the light, or the length of the beam have to be right or what, but when the light hits it, the water glazes over and solidifies. I've been lucky enough to watch it happen a few times now. Over time, it starts to look like this one here. It turns color as it matures."

"And then it...hatches."

"Exactly, just like a butterfly."

"And what comes out is a...faerie." The cogs in my brain were jamming up over it. Did I believe? I stared at the delicate cocoon and chewed my lip. There was nothing about it that looked artificial. It was when I noticed its translucency, that I could see shadows of the leaves behind it, that I did believe. Is there a moment when faith kicks in? I think yes, after this experience. There is a line to cross when the unbeliever becomes the believer. Some of us just need stronger evidence than others, but we all have that line inside us. As I passed my hand behind the cocoon and saw my shadow through it, my need was met. I believed.

"Aye. Amazing isn't it?"

"What does it look like?" I felt like someone had removed colored glasses from my face that I didn't know I had been wearing, and I'd just learned that grass was blue, not green.

Jasher caught my eye and smiled. I won't hide my feelings, the expression warmed me to my bones. "You'll be able to see it for yourself pretty soon if we get the timing right. At least, I reckon if you can see the cocoon, you'll be able to see the spirit that comes out too."

"Spirit?"

"Aye, they look more ghostly than flesh and blood. Transparent-like, you know?"

I looked at him. They looked more like ghosts. *He would know.* "What do they do?"

He shrugged. "Mostly they vanish into the plants and earth. Make things grow. Clean things up, become part of the energy that powers the forces of nature. They don't stick around. Once they drop, I almost never see them again, just a flash here and there."

"So the natural stuff around us is chock full of fae?"

"Sounds funny, I know. But everything has energy, right? Even the ancient Celts believed in animism."

I knew that word from my religion class last year. "Everything has a living spirit. Trees, the land, rocks..."

"Right. I've seen them disappear not only into plants, but into the ground and into stone. We think of stone as something inanimate, but when you see a spirit go into one, well, it's hard not to think of it as alive."

I became conscious of how close our faces were. When he spoke, a few wisps of my hair moved in his breath. That simple connection served to ground me, and my soul reached for it. We grasp at the tangible when the earth under our spiritual feet shifts unexpectedly.

"Can you..." he started, but stopped. "Do you..." he stopped again.

I waited. He looked more awkward that I'd ever seen him. This was a totally new Jasher to me and it was a little jarring. Suddenly, I knew what he was trying to ask. "See ghosts?" I supplied. He nodded but I shook my head. "No. I never have."

His face fell. "How did you know what I was trying to ask then?" Understanding dawned a second later. "Faith told you."

"Are you mad?"

He canted his head. "I might have been." He looked back at the cocoon and I followed his gaze. The purple droplet shimmered as the sky above the greenhouse brightened, and the driving rain eased a little. "But, no."

Not anymore. We'd found ourselves with a kinship, something he'd neither expected nor looked for. *I've never met anyone else who can see them,* he'd said.

"So, you're not weirded out?" he asked. Only then did I realize that he was just as concerned about what I thought, as I was about what he thought of me knowing. "It doesn't scare you?"

"Scare me?" My brows shot up. "I'm not the one who can talk to the dead, you are. Why would I be scared?"

"I don't know." He shrugged, looking uncomfortable. "My da wasn't so keen on it."

Something snapped into clarity, like the moment the view in your binoculars goes from fuzzy to sharp. His own father had rejected him, calling him a child of the devil. He'd been beaten and abused and abandoned, all because of things beyond his control. It made sense that Jasher expected rejection from me. With the exception of Faith, rejection was all he'd known.

"Your father didn't do right by you, Jasher." I sort of blurted this, not my most tactful moment, I'll agree. After all, it really was not my business. He gave me a look I couldn't define. I cleared my throat. "So, when will it hatch?"

We crouched so close I could see the detail of the five o'clock shadow hugging his chin and mouth. I wondered what it would feel like scraping against my face. I'd never kissed anyone with so much serious stubble before. I know, but these are the thoughts of a teenager. I was *really* having issues thinking of Jasher as my cousin. I wondered how he thought of me. I pulled my eyes away, but every nerve remained aware of him.

"It's hard to predict exactly, but they seem to vary between eighteen and twenty-two days. This one should drop in the next ten to twelve days."

I stared at the cocoon, mystified. "I'm going to camp out right here."

He laughed and stood. "We've got a couple days to go yet. Don't worry," he winked. "I won't let you miss it."

The friendly gesture looked bizarre on him. Understandable, since he'd been nothing but rude since I'd arrived.

"Does this have something to do with why you yelled at me like a jerk when I approached the greenhouse with my cell phone the other day?"

He grinned sheepishly and ran a hand through his hair. "Cell phones kill faerie cocoons. Get within a few meters and poof." He mimicked a little explosion with his fingers. "They turn to vapor."

"Why?" I said, alarmed.

He shrugged. "Radiation? Electromagnetic frequency? Your guess is as good as mine, but I don't think technology in general is good for young fae. I've never seen a cocoon form anywhere near power lines, cities, cell phone towers, or the like."

"This is why you don't have wifi, or electricity on this side of the house. I thought you were just a cave man." I looked down at the cocoon. "But really, you're protecting them."

He nodded. "I don't think it matters so much when they get a little older, but they're fragile at this stage. Like we all are when we're young."

I looked at him thoughtfully, taking in the soft brown eyes, the line of concern between his brows, the shadow of his lashes across his cheek. He had experienced a traumatic birth and an unspeakable childhood up until Faith had taken him in. It was no wonder he was so passionate about making sure that the fae survived. He caught me staring and looked me in the eye. We held each other's gaze for a fraction too long, seeing something there that connected us. For the first time since I'd met him, I finally felt like I was worth something to him.

Two little bulls of emotion smacked skulls inside me. One of them was happy and grateful that I'd finally gotten through to Jasher and made a connection, the other resented the fact that I had to say the magic password before he let me into the clubhouse. Shouldn't he have let me in just because I was a human being and part of his family? Finally, the bull with the word 'grateful' branded into its hide lifted its head, triumphant.

CHAPTER 13

The Criterion Café became my favorite place in Anacullough to answer my emails, surf the web, and otherwise lose myself in digital heaven. I had explored the Ana library and a few other locations, but the Criterion was roomy and had big windows at the front. The place always smelled like cinnamon buns and coffee, and I indulged in both a couple of times a week.

After the discovery of the fae, the energy between Jasher and me had warmed up impressively. When the door chimed at the Criterion and I looked up to see him enter, I smiled and waved. He grinned and weaved his way through the tables toward me.

I snapped my laptop closed.

"You really are addicted to this business, aren't you," Jasher said, gesturing at my computer. "Can't live without it."

"Don't you slander my beloved technology," I sniffed with false pretension. "At least I can hide from your judgemental gaze at The Criterion. How did you find me here?"

"Bike," he said, peering into my coffee cup and then taking a sip.

"Right." Faith's bright yellow townie was parked in the rack out front, screaming my whereabouts from the street like a neon sign. "What's up?"

I leaned my elbows on the table and caught a couple of young women noticing Jasher from another table.

"What are you smiling at?" Jasher asked, looking around.

"Nothing," I said, biting my cheeks. "What was so important that you came to find me?"

"I didn't come find you. I was just in the area."

"I see."

He shifted in his seat, lifted his ball cap off his curls and ran a hand through his hair. "Faith mentioned..." he cleared his throat.

I smiled again. He pronounced Faith as 'Fate'. It tickled me.

"What are you grinning at now?" he said, exasperated.

"Nothing. You're cute. Go on," I said.

"Dear God in heaven," he muttered, rolling his eyes, but his cheeks had taken on a pleasurable pink cast. "As I was saying, Faith mentioned that you haven't had much of the Irish experience so far, and that you might want to... get out and mingle with the locals, so to speak."

"She did?" I lifted my elbows off the table in surprise.

"Aye, she did." The pink color in his cheeks deepened. "She mentioned the Eithne summer party and..." he paused, looking embarrassed.

"Why, Jasher Sheehan," I put a hand to my heart. I batted my eyes and put on my finest Southern drawl. "Are you proposin' to take my otherwise lonely self to a soiree to mingle with all the finest folks of Anacullough?"

"Stop that."

"Why I never been asked to a summer ball by a man so fine as yourself," I tilted my head and fanned my face. "I'd be honoured to attend this famous Eithne ball..."

"It'll be a mud pit," he deadpanned. "You'll have to wear wellies." His eyes were at half-mast like an annoyed Garfield and I laughed at his expression. He stole another sip of my coffee and dimpled at me. "You're ridiculous."

"I know. So when's this party? Do we have to bring anything?"

"This weekend. You might want to wear a burka and bring a stick to fend off the boys." He stood.

"Nonsense. That's what you're for," I smiled up at him. It was the only compliment I'd ever received from him. I'd take it. "That's really all you came for, huh?"

"Aye. I was on my way to the lumber yard."

"Well, don't let me hold y'all up," I drawled.

He rolled his eyes again, but he was smiling. "See you later."

I watched the girls watch Jasher leave. They both cast curious looks at me. I opened my laptop and hid my smile behind my coffee cup.

* * *

THE NIGHT of the party was cool and overcast. It had rained most of the day but had tapered off toward evening. The streets were damp and there was a misty glow around the streetlights as Jasher parked his truck along the curb.

"Where's the party?" I asked, looking around. It looked like we were in a suburb.

"Through there," Jasher pointed to a set of tall, crooked gates. I couldn't see anything over the stone wall on either side.

"That looks seriously creepy," I said cheerfully as I unbuckled my seatbelt.

"It's in a park near the ruins of an old fortress called Eithne. The kids are allowed one party a year in there, as long as the place is spotless by morning."

I raised an eyebrow. "Irish teenagers are more responsible than Canadian ones if they clean up after a bush party."

"They lose the right otherwise." Jasher opened the truck and got out. The sound of rock music drifted over the stone wall. Jasher closed the door and came around to my side. "So far I guess they've held up their end."

"Do you come every year?" I closed my door and zipped up my wind breaker. I was carrying a bag of chips to donate to the snack table, and a couple of bottled drinks for us. Jasher's version had alcohol, mine didn't, thanks to Faith. Drinking in public was allowed in Ireland, but you had to be eighteen. I wondered if they enforced it. I followed that thought up with wondering what Jasher was like after he'd had a few.

"Gads no," Jasher said as we walked toward the open gate. "Once was enough for me. I haven't been to Eithne since I was sixteen."

I stopped walking just outside the gate. "What?" My shoulders slumped and I stared at him. "You don't even want to be here. Why did we come?" I turned and started back toward the truck.

Jasher grabbed my arm, laughing. "No, Georjie. It's alright. It'll be fun."

I turned back, shooting him a dubious look.

"We're here," he said. "Let's just go. You can't go back to Canada without having gone to an Irish party."

I let him steer me through the gates. I was frowning, and considering protesting again when the music got louder and the sound of good-natured laughter rolled over us.

"Whoa," I breathed, as we passed a cluster of trees and the scene opened up before me.

"See," said Jasher, behind me. "Worth it."

The black void of the park had a small but bright galaxy of light in the middle of it. Tall trees towered on either side, their shadows blotting out the sky to the left and right. Christmas lights had been strung up haphazardly across a stone square, roughly the size of a swimming pool. The lights criss-crossed in all directions, with no rhyme or organization, illuminating the people dancing and chatting below. A DJ spun from a low wooden stage, the large screen behind him displaying psychedelic animation.

It was the backdrop to this affair that made my jaw drop. Behind the partiers was the looming, rugged shape of a castle ruin. Two huge towers, each with a drunken lean toward each other, stood stark and black against the evening sky like rugged giants on watch.

"That's Eithne?" I asked.

"Aye, they're not actually allowed to cross that fence." Jasher pointed to a thick line of chain just behind the stone square. "There's always a spy here from the village, probably more than one. None of them know who it is, and it's someone different every year."

We walked up the gravel trail through the trees and the faint smell of beer hit my nose. "How old are most of these kids?" The soft gravel crunched underneath our feet, sinking into the wet soil.

"Up to twenty-five, I guess," Jasher said. "You'll be able to pick out the cliques soon enough."

He was right. When I really looked, it wasn't hard to see that the smooth-faced boys and soft-cheeked girls were hanging out together on the dance floor, while bearded men chatted up women who looked several years old than me.

"Jash?" A voice brought our attention to the side of the crowd furthest away from the DJ. A copper-haired guy strode toward us with a surprised smile. People behind him were looking over at us and talking.

"Colin," Jasher said, and the two shook heartily.

"Didn't expect to see you here. You haven't been to Eithne in years." Colin's eyes fell on me. "Who's this?"

"My c… a friend from Canada," Jasher said. The deliberate change in his choice of words wasn't lost on me.

"I'm Georjayna," I said. "I come bearing gifts." I lifted the bag of chips.

Colin gave a hearty laugh and threw an arm over my shoulder. "Welcome to Ireland," he said, exhaling the scent of beer over me and sweeping his other arm out. "Is it everything you dreamed of?"

I put on my best Irish accent. "Aye, there's good craic to be had, like. If I can get this one," I jerked my head toward Jasher, "to lighten up." The word 'craic' meant conversation, and that was pretty much the extent of my Irish-isms.

I winked at Jasher and he shook his head at me.

"Aye," his arm tightened, pulling my ear close to his mouth. He pointed his beer bottle toward Jasher and said conspiratorially, "This one was never out playin' t'under and lightning with us when we was kids, everyone thinks he's a bit touched in the head. But I know," he brought the beer bottle against his chest, "he's solid. Give me work when I was down, so he did."

Colin rattled off the names of his friends by way of introduction, pointing the neck of his bottle at them in turn. Most of them had accents so strong and spoke with so much slang that I had a hard time understanding them. I strained to pick up some of the funnier sayings, but failed most of the time.

Jasher propped himself up on the low stone wall and chatted with some of the guys, his own accent getting thicker, too. It was nice to see him relax for once.

My eyes wandered up to the ruin as I drank my cider and listened to the music.

"Fascinatin', isn't she?" came a feminine voice at my elbow.

I turned to a girl with short blonde hair whose head reached the vicinity of my chin. "Bea..." I started, then stopped, knowing I was going to get her name wrong.

"Emily," she smiled. "I did a project on Eithne in grade school," she said as we wandered closer to the ruin. "I was obsessed. You see that bronze plaque there?"

I did. It looked to be a memorial of sorts, with an inscription etched into the metal surface.

"I memorized every name on that plaque, and what happened here in 1556."

"What happened here?" I looked up at the two crumbling towers.

"A siege." Her voice took on a mesmerizing lilt. "These were tower-keeps. They were once about eighty-five feet high, and there were more of them, four total, but they were destroyed."

"Who was doing the sieging?" The moon was nearly full and had begun to rise over the ruin, dusting the disintegrating rock with cold blue light.

"Who else? The English. The siege only lasted two days. There were about fifty Irish holding the fortress, and a dozen Spaniards. There were some women and children, too."

"How many English?"

"Six hundred," she said.

We stood next to the thick chain, with the memorial just on the other side.

"That's hardly a fair fight. But the Irish won, right?" I expected a heroic underdog story but Emily was shaking her head.

"No. History doesn't work like the movies. For six hours each day, Eithne was bombarded by cannons. A demi-cannon can blast through thick stone if fired right. The English threw up assault ladders, and the Spanish would toss them off while the Irish threw down boulders and fired guns. They say the moat was full of wreckage and bodies and the walls of Eithne ran with blood."

My skin prickled. I imagined I could hear the sounds of cannon fire, screaming women, and crumbling stone.

"On the second day, the other two towers cracked and the great wall between them crumbled, crushing dozens and destroying their protection. The rest tried to flee but were gunned down or put to sword."

"Women and children, too?" I asked, horrified.

"No," she shook her head and turned to face me in the moonlight. "They were hanged."

I swallowed. "Lovely story for a party night."

"Aye, its not a happy one. But if we don't remember them, who will? That's why I memorized the dead." She looked up at the moon and began to list old-world Gaelic names off on her fingers. "Ó Cuinn, Mac Domhnaill, Ó Baoill, de Paor, Mac Catháin, Ó Cionga, Ó Ruairc. I could go on,"

"That's okay," I said. "I should get back to Jasher. Thank you for the history lesson. I'm thoroughly creeped out now."

She laughed, "Sorry. I do get passionate about my history. This wasn't just the story of a siege, it was strategically significant in the sixteenth century."

We turned and walked back to the party together. "How so?" I scanned the faces for Jasher.

"Once the English knew the tactics that broke through the fortress defenses, it was just rinse and repeat. The garrisons at Newcastle,

Rathkeale, Ballyduff and others all fell the same way. That's when guerrilla warfare came on the scene."

"Fascinating," I said, but I wasn't listening anymore. I spotted Jasher and my blood went cold. Something was wrong. His face was pale, and his eyes darted around, registering things I couldn't see.

I swore. "I'm so stupid," I whispered. "We're so stupid." I dropped my cider into a nearby can and strode through the crowd toward Jasher. "Sorry Emily, gotta run."

"Oh... kay..." she said behind me, confused at my abruptness.

People were talking to Jasher and he was making an effort to stay focused on them but failing. From the way his distraction shot from one place to another, it was clear he was being harassed by more than one entity.

"What's the matter with ye, Jasher" Colin said just as I pushed my way into the group. "Ye look like ye've seen a ghost."

I put my hands on Jasher's knees. "Jasher," I said, and his unfocused eyes snapped to me like I'd just materialized out of nowhere.

His eyebrows shot up, and relief flooded his face. "Georjie," he croaked.

"What the..." I started, then I stopped and took a breath. Heat flushed up my neck, and I swallowed down my frustration. "Sorry guys," I turned to the group and forced a smile. "Lovely to meet you. I've come down with a headache," I put my fingers to my temple. "Jasher, can you take me home?"

The whole performance reeked of poor acting but I didn't care - all I cared about was putting a stop to the look on Jasher's face.

He hopped down and took my hand. "Of course."

We said quick goodbyes to Colin and his friends and strode toward the gate, me pulling Jasher behind me.

Jasher began to mutter in Gaelic and the sound made my skin crawl with a million ants. He wasn't speaking to me.

"Are they going to follow you?" I asked.

He kept speaking in Gaelic, with a borderline pleading tone. It wasn't until we were inside the truck and had shut the door that he said, "No. Thank God they don't move very fast, and they don't stray far from their haunts."

"How many?"

Jasher didn't answer. I looked over at his pale face, his brow beaded with sweat.

"Jasher!"

"I'm thinking! Uh...seven," He raked a hand through his hair and let out a deep shuddering breath. "Yeah, seven." He looked over at me and suddenly grinned. "Don't be upset, Georjie. I'm used to it. Well, maybe not seven at once, but—"

"Why did you even take me there? You know about Eithne, don't you?" My heart was pounding with frustration.

"Aye, we study it in school," he said, turning the truck through the main intersection of Ana and heading towards home.

As we took the corner I spotted a man just outside the circle of light thrown by a streetlamp. He wasn't much more than a silhouette in clothing that looked too big for him. A newsboy cap was propped off-kilter on his head, and there was something familiar about it. There was also something off about the way he was moving, like a stiff animated scarecrow, or a zombie. I craned my neck as we went by, trying to figure out what made him familiar, but he was behind us and out of sight in a moment. I shook my head and turned back to Jasher, focusing on our own problem.

"I'm an idiot for letting you take me there," I said.

"Easy, Georjie," Jasher said, his voice now calm. We pulled to a stop at the last set of lights before our country road. "It's my fault, not yours. No need to be angry."

"I'm not angry," I said, my face relaxing a bit. "More scared from the look on your face, and creeped out."

"Aye, maybe it was stupid. I just wanted you to take more memories home with you than gardening," he gave a dry laugh.

"Oh, don't worry. I will," I said, shivering and remembering the sound of his voice, murmuring in Gaelic to beings I couldn't see.

"Usually, there's only one or two out around Eithne." He shuddered. "I wonder why there were so many out tonight?"

"The pounding music and the crowd might have had something to do with it," I muttered, still steaming. "What did they want?"

"What they always want," Jasher said as we approached Sarasborne and turned into the dark yard. "To be heard. Favors."

"Favors?" I asked as we walked up the path toward the dark house.

"Aye, strange things. They want you to get a message to their relatives, who are in fact dead themselves, or to dig something up they buried, or do things that make no sense at all, like attend a concert on their behalf."

"What?" I stopped halfway up the walk. "Why?"

"Who knows, Georjie?" He sighed, and I saw the exhaustion hanging on him like a heavy coat. His handsome face looked drawn and off-color. "Let's focus on life instead," he said, taking my hand and squeezing my fingers. "We've got a greenhouse with life in it, and we're going to be there when it hatches. Now shush," he said as we entered the mudroom. "Faith is a light sleeper." He stopped and looked at me in the gloom. "Maybe, don't tell her what happened tonight," he whispered.

"Why not?" Going to the party was Faith's idea.

"She'll feel terrible. She doesn't know the... extent of it. I never talk about them with her anymore, so it's my fault for lulling her into a sense of security."

I agreed to his request and didn't probe him for more about the ghosts, but I also did a lot of tossing and turning that night.

CHAPTER 14

As the days passed and the horrible night of the party fell into the past, Jasher and I became more excited for the big moment when the fae would hatch. The house found its rhythm and I began to feel like I belonged. Most mornings, I was up early and out for a run before seven and back for my shower by eight and then breakfast. I have never been a fan of breakfast. I rarely wake up hungry and I prefer dinner type foods, but Faith changed all that. Her piping hot scones fresh from the oven were to die for. She made delicious pancakes, the perfect soft-boiled egg, and beautiful fruit salads that included edible flowers. She single-handedly vaporized the stereotype of boring Irish cooking.

I had more strange dreams, all feeling like episodes from the same show, and each time it happened I would wake fuzzy and grasping to remember. By the time lunch rolled around, I'd forget them almost completely.

I almost never saw Jasher at breakfast. He's an early riser, and by early I mean disgustingly early. He was up and out of the house by five thirty a.m. He went to work in the morning and was back by three. He sometimes napped in the afternoon, always outside in a hammock, unless it was raining. I was intimidated at how much he could accomplish in one day and it pushed me to do more with my time. I worked on my photo composition course at The Criterion. I'd update my social platforms, check email, and indulge in my guiltiest pleasure - shopping online.

In the afternoons, I would help Jasher with one of his projects or take Faith's townie out to run an errand for her. Sometimes Jasher and I would go into Ana together. He'd go to the lumber yard and hardware store while I browsed antique shops. We always had to agree on a time to meet up because Jasher didn't carry a phone. I teased him about living in the dark ages, but inside, I appreciated his commitment to living a tech-free life. It was something I knew I could never do. My tech meant I could touch base with my friends whenever I missed them.

I'd help Faith in the garden, pulling weeds, deadheading, and pruning. It was while helping Faith weed one day, that the signs of a transformation began to whisper at the edges of my consciousness. It wasn't jarring, but it was also impossible to ignore.

I put my fingers on a plant, feeling the soft hairs on the leaves with the pads of my fingers. "Comfrey," I said. "Good for bone repair."

Faith, weeding nearby, looked up. "How did you know that?"

I frowned. "You must have told me." But, I couldn't actually recall her telling me about this particular species. I chalked it up to a mystery of the mind. Sometimes you just know things but don't know how you learned them. Faith shook her head like she couldn't recall telling me either, and went back to her work.

The grounds of Sarasborne were huge and there was always work to do, although I think Jasher thought of it as his playtime. He'd long since finished the renovation on the greenhouse roof and had started building the addition - a lab of sorts for Aunt Faith.

Faith usually joined me for breakfast and then left for the morning to visit clients. Sometimes she'd be gone all day but she'd spend a couple of hours every day out in the gardens and in her workshop.

On one of my morning runs, my eye caught on several tall plants with short stalked flowers clustered on the branches. Again, I knew the plant. Why did I know this plant? I stopped jogging and stepped into the ditch to examine it. I touched a leaf and bent to smell it when information zinged through my fingertips and into my mind. Burdock - a blood cleanser, a powerful detoxifier. The medicinal properties and chemical makeup of the plant filled my mind. I let go of the leaf, but the knowledge stayed. I shook my head. Aunt Faith must have told me about this plant while we were gardening, I just couldn't remember it. I backed away and continued my run. It seems daft that I rationalized it away like that, now that I look back. But that's what we do when something makes us uncomfortable - we rationalize.

But as I jogged down the driveway back to the house, it happened again. I passed a cluster of long stemmed plants with small yellow flowers. I stopped and looked at the tiny, daisy-like blossoms. The side door to the house opened and Faith came out carrying a bucket of compost.

"Morning Georjie. How was your run?"

"You've got Jacobaea Vulgarus growing there," I said, pointing. "It's deadly." I didn't even need to touch it to know.

Faith gave a surprised laugh. "Yes, but most people call it ragwort. Or even better," she cocked an eyebrow, "mare's fart." She threw fruit and veggie cuttings into the composter behind the garage. "I keep it for the pollinators."

I nodded. Thirty-two species of endangered insects feed on ragwort nectar. It's their only food source. I blinked, trying to remember how I knew that. I must have learned about it in school at some point.

"Come on in for breakfast," Faith said. She went back inside with her empty compost bucket.

I followed her inside. "Are you all packed for Aberdeen?"

"Aye." Faith picked up a pair of potholders and opened the oven. The smell of fresh scones wafted out. "You going to miss me?"

I took a big whiff and groaned with pleasure. "Nah. Just your baking."

She laughed and flicked me with the tea towel.

"Are you excited for your course?" I asked.

"Very." She scooped a scone up with a spatula and put it on a plate, then handed it to me. "When I left nursing to work on my own, I promised myself I'd do a course every year. It's a present to me."

"Now look who's the keener," I said, buttering the scone and watching it melt.

A look of guilt crossed Faith's face. "You guys will be okay?"

"Ha! If you'd asked me that when I first arrived, I would have clung to your leg and begged you not to leave." I shrugged. "Jasher and I made peace. You don't need to worry."

Her face relaxed. "Thank God."

I smiled. "Just enjoy your course. You're going to miss the fae hatching, though."

She shrugged and looked wistful. "I can't see them anyway. You can tell me all about it when I get back."

Every day after breakfast I went to look at the cocoon. I examined it carefully for hairline cracks and color changes. I was drawn to it as though there was an invisible elastic between us.

I had been wrestling with myself about telling my friends about all of this – the fae, the ghosts that Jasher could see. How do you explain supernatural things like that to someone who can't and probably never will see such a thing? They'd all think I was a nut. Maybe not Targa, she was pretty open minded. But I broke into a clammy sweat when I thought about telling even her.

I wanted to take a photo of the cocoon, but there was no way I would ever take my phone into the greenhouse. I had a new respect for the tiny super-computer that I was so addicted to. I still took it with me on my runs because I loved snapping photos of the Irish countryside. But I never left it sitting out, and I never took it into the greenhouse or garden.

As the cocoon had deepened in color, I had started getting up earlier and earlier to check it. Soon I was checking it a dozen times a day, afraid that I was going to miss it. Jasher laughed at my eagerness but he frequented the greenhouse more often, too. It became our meeting place. When it finally happened, it was the day after Faith had left for Aberdeen and first thing in the morning. Along with all of the other odd bits of knowledge that had somehow found their way into my head, I woke early and knew it was about to happen.

CHAPTER 15

I sprang out of bed and padded down the stairs in my pajama shorts and tank top. I regretted not getting dressed when I saw Jasher seated on a short stool in front of the cocoon. He turned and smiled. He jerked his head at me, the masculine equivalent of crooking a finger. Apparently I wasn't the only one who woke up knowing the big event was upon us.

Jasher had set up a folding table and had a leather-bound sketchbook open to a blank page, as well as a bunch of oil pastels spread out in a tray beside him. He'd selected a number of pastels from the purple and red spectrum. I had never seen so many variations on a color before. "You're going to draw it?"

Jasher nodded. "Of course. It's tradition."

Something clicked into place. "You're the one who drew the little faerie on the envelope," I said.

Jasher gave me a vacant look, and then clued in. "Oh, the letter Faith wrote to your mom?" He grinned. "Aye, that was me. I'd forgotten about that."

I crouched near him and examined the cocoon. "There's a crack!"

Jasher clamped his teeth around his pencil and reached for another stool. He put it beside him and I took a seat. "It won't be long now. I was about to come up and get you."

We watched as the miracle unfolded before our eyes. The cocoon was open all the way down the middle now, and tiny movement was detectable. I felt as though frozen in time. The creature that emerged was exquisite. The purple color that had shown through the cocoon had clearly come from her wings and hair. A faint glow surrounded her, and I saw what Jasher meant about them looking almost like ghosts. I could see the outline of leaves behind her. She was delicate, and I shivered at the thought of what a cell phone could do to her. Her eyes were closed, her wings damp and creased. The cocoon was now a transparent shell as it opened away from her. Her limbs were folded in on herself and her head lay on her knees, her face toward us.

Jasher's pencil skimmed over the page, outlining her shape.

"You must have eyes like a hawk," I whispered as I watched her form come to life on the page. He was brilliantly skilled, and it didn't surprise me in the least.

"Better," he whispered back.

"Why are we whispering?"

"You started it."

The faerie unfolded and stretched her limbs and wings. Jasher sketched lightly and quickly, getting down her proportions and her shape. He froze when her eyes fluttered open for the first time. The black lashes were thick both above and below, the ones on the bottom were longer than the ones on the top, giving her face a melancholic quality. She was unafraid, inquisitive, and looked both juvenile and ancient at the same time. Her wings stretched.

Like a whisper in the back of my mind, I heard her name.

"Rasha," I said, softly. The faerie cocked her head toward me, and then nodded, almost deferentially.

Jasher's jaw dropped. "How did you know her name?"

"She said it, didn't you hear her?"

Jasher shook his head. "I didn't hear anything."

"I heard it." I took breath. Had I heard it, or had I thought it?

"Interesting," Jasher murmured. He scrawled her name on the top of the page and continued sketching. Her wings suddenly buzzed so fast that they were nothing but a blur of violet. Jasher's strokes became urgent. Less than a minute later, she flew between us in a blur and was gone - up and out the open dome.

Jasher continued sketching and adding color to his drawing. I watched over his shoulder as he finished it off. "You're really amazing. That was really amazing. I mean, the whole thing was just...amazing!"

Jasher gave me an enigmatic look. "Aye, I still get goosebumps."

"May I see some of your other drawings?"

He handed me his open sketchbook.

I laid it open on my lap, flipping back one page to the faerie before Rasha. He had a crazy shock of green hair that stuck straight up in a point, and black eyes that were smaller than Rasha's.

"Looks like this one happened in June, just before I came."

"Aye."

I wondered if Jasher's plan was to stay at Sarasborne and dedicate himself to landscaping and drawing fae for the rest of life. Did he want a family? Children? I wanted to ask, but didn't have the courage yet.

As I turned the pages, my respect for Jasher's talent grew. Page after page of beautifully rendered and exceptionally unique fae of all colors, shapes, sizes passed under my fingers. If I had found this sketchbook and not known who owned it, I would have said it belonged to an accomplished female artist. The delicate nature of the fae and the rainbow of colors seemed intrinsic to a woman's touch. If I hadn't watched Jasher sketch one right in front of me, I wouldn't have believed the images were his.

Who was this person? He was a rugged lover of the outdoors, a handyman with callouses. A work boot and glove wearing carpenter and landscaper. He could see spirits, something I'd never come across before, but he also had remarkable talents, both musical and artistic. Through his drawings shone a love for the little beings that was so poignant they made bare his heart. He was being as vulnerable with me in this moment as anyone could be. We both grew silent as I turned page after page. I was horrified to discover that there were tears behind my eyelids, threatening to fall.

"Georjayna?" Jasher said quietly.

I swallowed. I closed the sketchbook before I had finished looking at all of them because if I kept flipping, I was going to make a fool of myself. "They're incredible," I finally said, and cleared my throat. I handed him his sketchbook. "I could only ever dream of having a talent like yours."

We locked eyes. My cheeks heated but I didn't look away. His expression was unreadable, his gaze unwavering. Finally, I stood up a bit too suddenly. I turned away to give myself a moment to recover and asked the first thing that came to my mind.

"Why do you think the number of cocoons is shrinking?"

He shrugged. "It makes sense. Industry and technology are growing, so I suppose it's harder for them to make it through the chrysalis phase. They're just so fragile when they're young."

There was no stopping progress. At what point did our world become so toxic that fae couldn't make it through the chrysalis stage anymore? What would happen to the natural world then?

The high that I'd had from watching Rasha hatch had vanished. The world had enough environmentalists out there railing against industry, didn't it? I'd become numb to the need. I had been given a violent shove into reality.

Nature was not just a force outside myself that I could admire when the mood struck. Nature now had a face, a form and a heartbeat. It had a people. One that lived in near obscurity; one that was integral to our own survival but was slowly being exterminated.

CHAPTER 16

The next day, I was eating lunch alone in the gazebo when my phone lit up with a text.

Targa: *How's life with the troll?*

Me: *We've made peace, thank God. And I don't think he's crazy anymore.*

Targa: *No? Did you ask him about it after all?*

My fingers hovered over the keyboard, thinking. How should I answer this? I typed out: *He can see dead people.* But I didn't hit send, and a few seconds later I deleted it and wrote: *Just a misunderstanding.*

She took a second to write back.

Targa: *How evasive. Lucky for you I'm heading out to meet the salvage team at the beach just now or I'd needle you for details.*

Me: *You sound so professional.*

Targa: *Don't change the subject. You're telling me more later.*

Me: *Yes ma'am.*

I was halfway to the house from the gazebo when Jasher's work truck pulled into the driveway. He hit the brakes, spraying gravel. The engine was off and he was out the door in the same moment.

"Everything okay?" I called across the lawn.

"The greenhouse is open, yeah?" He slammed the truck door and jogged toward Sarasborne.

"Yes. I haven't closed it. Should we?" A few droplets of moisture hit my cheek and forehead.

"No, no," he exclaimed. "There's a storm coming. But not a violent one like the last time." His shoulders and hair did look damp, his dark curls clinging to his neck and forehead. "I just came from Ana, it's already raining there." His eyes were bright and hopeful.

"You think this storm might make a cocoon?" I looked up, doubtfully. The sky was a light shade of gunmetal, with a few scuds of cloud. A breeze tugged at my hair.

"We can hope. If we get rain and then the sun comes out..." He shrugged. "Maybe."

I left my cell on the kitchen counter as we dashed through the house and into the greenhouse. The first smattering of rain started to fall. We closed the glass doors that separated Faith's workshop from the plants, and put away a few random tools. The rain became heavier and the sky closed in with clouds. Jasher and I grinned at each other. Comrades.

"Nothing to do now but wait and see," Jasher said. He sat on the threshold of the greenhouse and parlor where there was no danger of getting wet. I parked myself in a chair near the sliding door. I tried to relax and enjoy the rain, but excitement thrummed through me and I chewed my thumbnail - a nervous tic I'd had since I was kid. Liz would have slapped my hand away.

Jasher laughed and I looked over. "What?"

"Your spine is ramrod straight. Try and relax. Most likely, nothing will happen."

But within a few minutes we were both pacing.

The rain lasted about an hour but it felt like days. By the time the driving pellets had eased, Jasher was sprawled on the sofa and I sat with my legs draped over the side of a chair reading a gardening book I'd grabbed from the shelf. I say reading when I really mean looking at pictures. Jasher lifted his head, fast. My head snapped up too. We were like a couple of hunting dogs hearing a twig snap in the woods.

He cocked his head. "I think it's stopping."

"So far so good, right? Look at all the raindrops." Every plant and leaf dripped with rainwater. The rain had now let up to a light sprinkle. Jasher stepped over the threshold and I followed. We peered up through the open dome. A few drops spattered my face. Gray clouds thickly blanketed the sky.

"Those have to break, now," Jasher said.

We watched as the rain slowed and then stopped. Leaves dripped rainwater into the soil, darkening it nearly to black. Jasher and I stood on the rubber mats so we didn't stir up mud. The light changed, brightened. A seam ripped through the clouds and the sun tried to poke through.

Jasher turned his gaze on me and gave me that heart-stopping grin. "It's perfect. We couldn't ask for better conditions than this." The clouds continued to break and beams of sunlight penetrated, finding their way to the earth.

Jasher commentated as we hovered like nervous parents. "The trick is that the drops have to not fall so fast," he lowered his voice nearly to a whisper. "They have to cling to a leaf for long enough for a beam of sunlight to penetrate them. I think, and this is just my guess, the light has to be the right temperature," Jasher said. "They don't happen on cold days. The combination has to be warm light and pure water. Think of the droplets as the egg and the sunlight as the sperm."

I couldn't help but laugh.

Jasher shot me a lopsided grin. "It's true," he said in mock defense. "It's nature's way, isn't it? Look now at how quickly the plants are dripping. In a few minutes there will be less water running off the leaves. Keep your eyes..."

He didn't have a chance to finish. A tiny sparkle like sunlight glinting off a lake flashed in the corner of my eye. "There!" I pointed.

A droplet had frozen over and turned pastel green. My pulse sped up. Another flash caught my eye as a second one formed on the same plant, only this one was pink.

"There," both Jasher and I said at the same time and then laughed. My heart felt light as a feather and I had a surreal thought flash through my mind. *This is happiness.*

Jasher clapped a hand to his forehead comically. "Two!"

"There," I gasped, pointing. A sparkle hanging from the top leaves of a potted basil plant glazed over to yellow.

"Janey Mack!" Jasher's voice was loaded with awe.

I laughed. "What does that mean?" But I could guess.

The greenhouse filled with twinkles, flashing like fireflies among the plants. The visual was pure magic. We fell silent, stunned. Colored cocoons were forming all over the greenhouse, on every plant. Jasher's mouth sagged open. This wasn't a bumper crop, it was a fully stocked terrarium. The hair on my arms stood up. The energy in the greenhouse was changing. I tuned in to the soles of my feet in my flip flops. A subtle hum of power had begun to thrum underneath me and the air crackled with energy.

"Do you feel that?" I put a hand on Jasher's arm.

"What?" he whispered.

"That vibration. The energy."

He gave a small headshake. "What vibration?"

"I don't know." I didn't know how to describe it.

The sun crawled behind the clouds and the cocoons slowed and then stopped forming as the light faded. I let go of his arm as Jasher stepped under the open dome and began a slow walk around. I followed in a daze. With every step, I could feel the energy beneath my feet, thrumming under my shoes. The sight of plants loaded with cocoons was fantastical. The air felt humid and clean and rich with natural perfume. Every plant dripped with transparent colored raindrops, frozen in time right before they were to fall.

"Unbelievable," Jasher whispered.

I felt very deeply that we were present, no, had somehow facilitated even, an event that may only happen once in a century. I was wrong about that.

* * *

LATE THAT NIGHT, the sound of a pounding of a hammer ripped me from my sleep. My heart vaulted into my throat and I gasped, nearly choking on my own tongue. I had been dead asleep and dreamless.

Tap. Tap. Tap.

It wasn't a hammer - there was knocking at my door. I rubbed the sleep from my eyes and looked at the clock. Two forty-three a.m. The full moon cast bright dappled shadows across the carpet. As the sleep fog cleared, I registered the sound of light rain and wind. A few raindrops spattered against the windows. I threw the covers back and padded to the door just as I heard two more taps.

"Georjie?"

I opened the door. Jasher's eyes were wide and bright like he was surfing a tidal wave of freshly brewed coffee.

"What's wrong?" I stifled a face-splitting yawn and covered my mouth. Both of my eyes sprang a leak.

"Sorry to wake you, but I thought you wouldn't want to miss this. Can you come down?" He didn't wait for my response, and vanished down the stairs.

I foraged on the floor with my toes for my slippers and spotted the faint white blobs peeking out from under my bed. After finding my robe, I wrapped it around me and left the room, raking the tangles from my hair. Rounding the corner at the bottom of the stairs, I paused and listened. Faint footsteps led to the greenhouse, so I followed Jasher there.

He sat on the threshold with the sliding doors open, his chin in his hands. I sat down beside him. There were no lights on and he didn't say anything.

"What's happen... Ohhhhh." A glimmer caught my eye, and then another. The clouds moved across the moon and its bright cool light illuminated the scene before us. More cocoons were forming, not as quickly as they had formed during the day, but they were still appearing faster than I could track them with my eyes. The foliage twinkled with what looked like colored fire flies.

"They can form in moonlight?" I whispered, amazed. "You never told me."

"I didn't know!" he whispered back, shrugging his shoulders up to his ears. "Georjayna," He put a hand on my forearm and peered into my eyes. "Moon fae," he said, drawing out the word 'moon.' A big grin split across his face.

"Moon fae." I grinned back.

We watched in silence for the next ten minutes as the little cocoons dropped. They soon slowed, and the twinkling lights stopped. The greenhouse became just a greenhouse on a moonlit night, the light changing as clouds slid across the moon's face. So, the event that I had thought would only happen once in a century, happened twice within a matter of hours.

CHAPTER 17

"You're really lucky, Georjie." Jasher's voice broke the stillness. I loved the sound of my nickname coming out of his mouth.

"Why?"

"This is your family's legacy," he said. "How many other families have this kind of connection with nature?"

"It's yours too, Jasher. You're part of this family."

He shrugged. "Yes and no. I know Faith wouldn't want me to feel anything other than part of this family, but I know where I came from and what I am."

"What do you mean 'what you are'? What are you, besides a Sheehan?" I turned to examine him in the dim light. There it was - the deep sadness I'd seen before in the photographs of him when he was young. It wasn't gone after all.

"Cursed."

"No Jasher, you're not cursed. You're blessed," I protested. But the memory of the party returned like a monster just under the surface of a black lake, and I knew I didn't really believe that.

He gave a humorless laugh. "I appreciate you trying to look at the bright side, but it's not a blessing when your mother dies while you're still inside her."

I blinked at his bluntness. He'd just opened the door wide and beckoned me to come in.

"I should be dead," he was saying. "Whatever force kept my mother's body going to birth me was not good. It wasn't a miracle. It branded me. It's not a blessing to be able to see and talk to the dead. The dead should be at peace, not wandering around harassing the living. And I should be among them."

My skin grew clammy. He believed his words wholeheartedly.

"I don't know what it's like to see and talk to the dead, Jasher," I began. "But anytime there is life where there could have been death, it seems like a miracle to me. If you have been marked because you came close to the veil between the living and the dead, then you are special."

"No, Georjie. What little good my ability does, is far too feeble for the price that I've had to pay for it. You don't know what it's like to have more interactions with dead people than living. I have a much less rosy view of humanity because of what the dead have admitted to me. They have no qualms about telling you everything they did while they were alive. They're all looking for redemption. When they find an ear, they won't leave you alone. Living people keep their secrets and take them to the grave, but once they're in the grave it's like they realize that the only way they'll feel better is by making sure they have no secrets left."

"You mean they tell you their life stories?"

"No, not their life story, if it was only that maybe I could bear it. They want to tell you their sins, ask you to do weird things for them. The ones like Conor are the nice ones who led good lives, and they're interested in being helpful. But most of them are not like that," he went on. "Most of them are the leavings of wretched humans who have nothing to offer the living except horror stories."

I understood why Jasher felt like he was cursed. I opened my mouth to thank him for telling me when he said, "And another thing. I'm not even so sure that most of the ghosts I've spoken with really are the ghosts of people."

"What else would they be?"

"Sometimes...sometimes it seems like no human being could ever be so wicked. They've done things that are beyond inhumane. The very word 'inhumane' means a lack of humanity."

"Can you give me an example?"

His mouth went flat and hard. "I don't want to put awful things in your head. But some of the things the dead admit to, with full detail and rich description, seem more like the acts of demons, not people."

"Do you mean they were possessed?" I asked.

"What else would you call it when a human being commits acts that are against humanity? Why would a human being ever do something evil, something that gains him nothing, if he hadn't lost control somehow of his own humanity?"

My mind went back to a horrific event that had happened in Canada when I was still in junior high school. "There was a man on a train once who attacked an innocent kid who was just listening to music. The man killed the kid...in front of everyone." I shuddered. "He showed no emotion while he was doing it, or so the witnesses said." I swallowed hard. Bile churned in my belly. It was an event that I could never forget. Kids had cried in the hallways at school after it hit the news. Some of them had been so disturbed they went home for the rest of the day.

"Exactly," said Jasher, quietly. "Things exactly like that. Do you think if that man had been in his right mind, he would have done that? He destroyed the life of that boy, the lives of everyone who witnessed it, the boy's family, and his own life. Why would any human in charge of all his faculties do that?"

"No, I think he was very, very sick," I agreed. "But I don't know about possessed."

"What is illness but a type of possession? Something unwelcome and unwanted that has a hold or a power over your body, no?" He cocked a dark eyebrow.

I began to see how he was looking at it, but I didn't know if I agreed. "You could put it that way." I have never been a philosophical person, and the stuff he was hitting me with was firing neurons that had never been fired before.

"Then what else is a demon but something that has more hold over you than you do? Anything from alcoholism to pneumonia to depression to mental illness."

"But are you saying that the people who are afflicted with these horrible things are faultless for their behaviors?"

"I don't know if I would use the word faultless," he said, frowning. "I think my experience with the dead makes me realize that human beings are not always responsible for what happens to them, but they are accountable for it. They are the ones who pay, whether they were under the influence of some other force or not."

I had never met anyone who thought the way Jasher did. I felt my understanding of the world being challenged, stretched. My perceptions of the nature of good and evil were widening but it wasn't without strain.

"My curse is why I'll never travel, never leave home." Jasher's voice was laced with bitterness, something I hadn't heard in his voice before.

This was what I was most interested in. I turned toward him. "Faith makes it sound like you prefer to be a homebody, like what makes you the happiest is working in the greenhouse or the backyard all by yourself."

"That's what you would do, too, if every time you went to a town or a city, the dead found you." He turned and looked me in the eye.

"So, what would you do with your life if you didn't have this curse?"

He laughed. "What wouldn't I do? I would go to University, probably study architecture. I would travel the world. Visit the Chinese temples in Paru and Panakha, go to Rome, Prague, Budapest, Angkor Wat. There's nothing that I wouldn't like to see with my own eyes. But the prospect of what would haunt me if I ventured out into the world is enough to make me want to crawl under my bed and never come out."

So there it was. He harbored much greater ambitions and desires than he had the courage to go after, because of a sight he didn't want to have.

I took his hand. "I'm sorry, Jasher. I didn't know."

He squeezed my fingers fiercely, hard enough to hurt. I could now see him as someone with real vulnerabilities and needs. We sat there, just holding hands. I felt a glowing warmth building in my belly like a breath blowing gently over hot embers.

"I've not shared that before," said Jasher. "I didn't mean to burden you."

I shook my head. "There is no true friendship without honesty." I shrugged nonchalantly. "Or so I've read."

He chuckled and turned my hand over, stroking my palm with the pad of his thumb. He looked into my eyes. He lifted his other hand, and traced my cheekbone with the finger. My pulse quickened at his touch. "And what about you, Georjie. What is it that you want? What did you come here for?"

I had a quick intake of breath. I hadn't expected to be asked that so bluntly. "Coming to Ireland happened by accident," I answered. My eyes dropped from his eyes to his lips. "But it doesn't feel like an accident anymore."

"No," he said. "It wasn't an accident." He kissed my temple, and put his arm around me. I lay my head on his shoulder and twined my fingers through his. The sounds of the night closed in around us, insects chirruping, the hoot of an owl. We shared a secret that, as far as we knew, couldn't be shared with anyone else. You might think that it was the perfect time and place for a kiss. Faith was away, we were alone in the house with a moonlit greenhouse full of fae cocoons spread out before us. But we didn't. Not then. It was more than romantic, it was spiritual. I never thought so before, but in that moment I realized - some moments didn't need a kiss to make them better.

CHAPTER 18

It was dusk. The day had been damp and hazy, the hottest since my arrival. Supper had been had, dishes washed, and the house was getting that feeling of evening stillness. I had just stepped out of the shower and wrapped my hair up in a towel when a couple of faerie names tinkled in my mind. I shook my head, thinking I'd imagined them.

I heard rapid footsteps on the stairs. "Georjie, you up here?" Jasher called.

I poked my head out the door. "In the bathroom. What's up?" More fae names snuck in through the back door of my consciousness.

I clued in to why I might be hearing fae names just as he said, "It's starting."

"I'll be right down!" I dressed frantically, pulling clothing over still wet skin, then ran down the stairs as quickly as Jasher had run up them. The fae names were whispering themselves into my mind and coming faster now. I was missing it.

Jasher was sitting in the same place as he had been when we had watched the moon fae form, with his legs out the patio door, on the top step.

"You're not going to go closer?" I plopped down beside him.

He shook his head. "Once they start, the best view will be from back here."

He was right. At first it was merely a twinkling, little flashes of white light. As the sun went down, the twinkling lights grew bright, and the soft pastel colors were detectable. The darkening greenhouse became our own personal solar system. It started slowly, but soon the sparkles were happening faster than we could spot them. The names chiming off quietly in my head became an endless stream of whispers as the fae introduced themselves to me.

"Can you hear them?" I asked Jasher.

He shook his head. "You can?"

I nodded. But I was too astounded for conversation and didn't say any more. The sight of the fae hatching was a laser-light show. Colors blinked and bright streaks shot around the greenhouse like tiny shooting stars.

"I wonder why they aren't leaving," Jasher said. "They always leave."

I got up and walked into the greenhouse, wanting to be closer to them. I walked slowly, tuning in to that inexplicable vibration humming under my feet. I stopped under the dome, open to the summer night sky. All around me twinkling lights zipped this way and that, blinking on and then going dark. Jasher joined me and the two of us stood under the open dome, silent. When the flashing, blinking, zipping lights stopped, we looked at each other in surprise.

As though someone had used a dimmer switch to turn them up, thousands of tiny lights illuminated fully and held steady. The twinkling lights lifted as each faerie hovered in the air. The spirits were so small that I couldn't make out anything other than a sparkle of light and the faintest fluttering of wings. The floating fae began to rotate around us, at first creating a cylinder spinning lights, but soon they broke into two swirling lines – a double helix. It was like an animated DNA strand I'd seen in a video in biology class once.

Every hair on my body stood on end. Jasher and I stood in the center of two sweeping spirals of light. That energy thrummed in the earth beneath us. The effect was beyond mesmerizing. The tiniest hairs on my body lifted in response to the soft wind the spinning fae created. Between the vibration under me, the fae sparkling around me, Jasher next to me, and the moon above me, I felt transported.

Jasher stepped closer and took me in his arms and we stood there wrapped up in one another. His warmth enfolded me. The swirling fae sparkled past my periphery as I looked up at him. He bent his head kissed me, and it seemed like the most natural thing in the world. His warm lips touched mine and my body melted into his. It wasn't a deep, passionate kiss; rather a sweet one, gentle. I didn't close my eyes, I didn't want to miss the twinkling stars sweeping by. He didn't close his eyes either, and his dark irises reflected the fae lights in their inky blackness. I was looking at a universe of shooting stars in his eyes. I wanted to fall right through and into them.

Jasher ended the kiss before I was quite ready. He pulled back and raised a hand to touch my face. "It's you," he said, so quietly I almost didn't hear. His arms tightened around me, pressing me close to his chest.

"What do you mean?" I whispered.

He released me and stepped back. The flying fae parted for him as he backed up, then they closed around me once again. The twinkling double-helix seemed to be never ending. I didn't know what to do to acknowledge them, so I just lifted my arms out, making a sort of scarecrow, palms up. The tiny lights began to leave the double-helix to land on me. A warm rush went through me and my heart rate doubled. Feather-light touches all over me made me gasp. Lights floated in front of my face and then landed there too, winking on my cheeks and blurring my vision.

"Jasher," I gasped, and looked for him. I could barely see him. The twinkling lights so close to my eyes made him look dark and fuzzy.

"Georjie," Jasher's voice was awestruck. "What I wouldn't give for a camera right now."

I held my hands out in front of me. I looked absolutely coated in miniature Christmas lights. My sensitive scalp, still damp from my shower, detected the tiny whirring fans of their wings as they fluttered against my head. I looked down at my body. Every surface of me was wrapped with fae. I was a human form made of light. I barely dared to breathe.

"Why?" I exhaled the question lightly.

"Ask them," suggested Jasher. "Rasha told you her name, maybe they'll tell you what they want."

"Can I help you?" I asked, looking down at the lights covering my body.

Tiny bells went off in my head, thousands of them - all whispering the same word.

Wise. Wise. Wise. Wise. Wise. Wise. Wise.

"What did they say?" Jasher asked.

I looked up, puzzled. "Nothing that made any sense."

The lights lifted and began to swirl again, and this time they spiraled up and out of the dome to be swallowed by the night.

The magical moment was over so unexpectedly that it left me feeling bereft and wishing I had paid more attention. And isn't that the way the most precious moments of our lives come and go? They're over in a moment leaving us breathless and dizzy, and feeling like yelling 'Wait, don't go!'

Every name I heard that evening was seared into my memory. I could have written them all down and not missed a single one.

CHAPTER 19

I stepped out of the Ana County Library and onto the stone steps. After the fae hatched, I began to look a lot harder for answers. I had been researching faeries, trying to unearth clues about why they had targeted me, and why they might have said the word *Wise* in answer to my question. It had been an afternoon of fruitless reading. I had seen some beautiful pictures, some of which may have been done by artists who actually knew what fae looked like, but most of it was pure mythology.

A man rounded the corner of the library and my eyes and thoughts were arrested by him. I had seen him before but it took a moment to come to me. It was Brendan, the man Faith and I ran into on the street on my first day. I narrowed my eyes. He moved just like the man I'd seen on the street the night of the party, and in fact wore the same newsboy cap. He looked ghastly, much worse than when I'd first seen him. He'd lost weight. Dark bags circled his eyes, and patchy beard growth gave him a careless, unwashed appearance. He also looked angry, sort of like an underweight pissed off bear who just woke up to discover he's overslept and starving to death.

Brendan's angry eyes hit on me briefly, but the hatred in his expression turned my blood to ice. There was madness there. He bared his teeth as he passed, shuffling like he had a bad hip. He hadn't had a bad hip when I'd first met him, not that I could recall. I stood still as he passed, not wanting to do anything to poke the bear. Eyes narrowed, I watched him make his way to the intersection. It had to have been him that I saw under the streetlight the night of the party.

As he reached the curb, a pedestrian appeared around the corner of the library and the two smacked into one other with an audible 'oooof' from the pedestrian. He was a large man in his own right, but the impact was a hard one.

It wasn't the collision that made me stumble back and stifle a cry of fear. It was the three dark bat-like creatures that exploded from Brendan's body. They flapped wildly around both men, all sharp edges and trailing spectral smoke. I could see the steeple of the church in the distance as one wispy body passed in front of it. The three dark shapes swirled in the air, looking disoriented, and then disappeared back into Brendan's body as he righted himself and carried on without apology. The pedestrian straightened his hat and jacket, mumbled to himself, and continued on. He had not seen what I'd seen.

I sucked in a breath and stared after Brendan as he crossed the street, watching for the dark creatures, my eyes straining. They had appeared as clear as day to me, but no one else on the busy street seemed to have noticed a thing. Brendan turned the corner; only then, when he was out of view, did I realize my heart was racing. My mouth was filled with chalk and I was sweating like someone on a gallows, the noose being slipped about their neck. The day was warm but my fingertips had gone ice-cold. Surely those creatures hadn't been real? But fae were real, and I could see them. So what were the nasty looking things using Brendan as a bat-cave?

"Are y'all right, Miss?"

I turned to see a skinny man carrying a bag of groceries in one arm. I don't remember sitting down, but there I was, perched on the edge of a library step, gaping. I shut my mouth.

"I'm okay." I wasn't, though.

"G'day to you then." He tipped a finger to the brim of his cap and moved along.

My phone chirped and I fished it out of my bag. It took me a second to register the name, which was a really bad sign because it was Liz.

I closed my eyes and tilted my head back. *Patience.* Since I'm trying to be honest here, I'll say that I hadn't spared a single thought for Liz since the day of search and destroy. Seeing her name felt like; *Who is this? I have a mother?* Apparently, even though I hadn't thought of her much, the irritation associated with Liz was right there just below the surface because it sprang out in full force like a spitting cat from a dark alley.

"Hello," I answered, my heart heavy with dread. I didn't want to talk, but we were way beyond due to touch base. If I didn't answer, she'd just call Faith.

"Hi, Poppet!" She sounded so enthusiastic that I pulled the phone away and gawked at it. I put it back to my ear. "How are you? How is your visit going?"

"It's fine." *I just saw some horrifying demon-bats fly out of a man. And I can see faeries. Have you ever seen a faerie, Liz?* Obviously, I didn't say any of that. And if you think I'm a wise-ass and should respect my mother, you're right, but I wasn't feeling it at the time.

"What are you doing?" she asked.

"Just running some errands." My voice was cool, clipped. Somehow, I couldn't change my tone, it was stuck in one runner.

"What's Jasher like? Are you getting along?" Her voice also seemed stuck a half-octave higher than normal. Strange.

"He's great. Listen, it's kind of a bad time, I'm just about to bike home."

"Oh."

She was disappointed. Even stranger. Did she have something to tell me? Was it something about dad? "What's going on? Everything okay?"

"Yes, everything is okay. I'll let you go. I just..." There was a pause so long I thought we'd dropped the call. "I just miss you," Liz said.

I blinked. Liz missed me? I couldn't even remember the last time I'd heard those words from her, now they were so unused they sounded like a foreign language. I filled the dead air with what I was supposed to say. "Miss you too, Liz. Gotta run though. Thanks for calling."

"Okay, call when you can. Love you."

I shook my head like a dog trying to oust a high pitched sound. Liz and I hadn't said 'I love you' to one another since...when? We didn't say 'I love you.' I heard 'I love you' more often from my friends. I opened my mouth, but the words backed up in my throat like a person afraid of heights being pushed to jump out of a plane.

There was a click in my ear. She'd hung up. I pulled the phone back and gazed at it.

I put my cell away and memories of the smoky-bats crowded out any more thoughts of Liz. Feeling dazed, I retrieved the yellow townie from the bike rack, threw a leg over it, and pedaled for Sarasborne.

CHAPTER 20

That afternoon found Jasher and me walking the back of the property. I'd wanted to take a closer look at the bridge, so I'd taken my camera outside to snap some photos. Jasher had pulled into the driveway for his lunch break and I waved to him. He came ambling over the lawn to join me. We hadn't seen each other since the double-helix kiss. My fingers went a little clammy as he approached. Would things be awkward between us now?

He looked relaxed and a touch pink from the sun. "Morning, Georjie," he said. "How did the fae's anointed sleep last night?"

"Ha!" I gave a sarcastic laugh. "Very funny." I had stooped to take a photo of a cluster of crocuses and stood. "Did you build that?" I pointed to the rustic old bridge. It was rough-hewn, with a short arch leading over a shallow burbling stream which ran across the back yard.

"No, that's been here for probably a hundred years," he said as he fell into step beside me. "I'm not sure which one of your ancestors built it, but they did a good job. Maybe not with the finishing of it, but it's sturdy."

We walked toward the bridge together.

The demon-bat things I had seen had been haunting me nonstop.

If anyone might know what they were, it would be Jasher. "Have you ever seen anything besides faeries or ghosts?" I asked.

His head inclined toward me. "Like what?"

I shrugged. "I don't know. Demons, or evil spirits?"

"And if I have?"

I looked at him curiously. He sounded more cagey than usual. Something I'd learned from having Akiko as a friend was that if I wanted her to be vulnerable, I had to be vulnerable first. It didn't always work, but it was always worth a shot. I cleared my throat. "I might have seen something."

He raised his eyebrows. "Such as?"

I told him. He listened quietly, and didn't show any real shock.

"I can't say I've seen anything like that specifically. I've seen some spirits of the dead that seem demonic. They don't fly around like bats but they surely don't look like something that I'd like to immortalize in a sketchbook."

My mind caught on that statement like the fabric of a shirt catches on a bramble. "Why *do* you draw the faeries?" I asked. "I mean, besides the fact that they're beautiful, and you can't take pictures of them."

A look of surprise crossed his face. "I thought you knew."

"No. Why, should I?" We stepped up onto the bridge and leaned our elbows on the railing. The creek burbled cheerily below us.

"Your family has been drawing the fae for a century and a half. Maybe longer. You really didn't know?"

"What?" This was a moment where I once again felt let down by Liz. She had never told me about any such tradition. It made me wonder what else she hadn't told me about our family, and growing up in Ireland. I'm not sure what startled me more - the fact that it had become a tradition and I didn't know about it, or the fact that there were more people in my family that could see the fae.

"Georjie, there's a cabinet upstairs in the library that is full to bursting with sketchbooks. I can't believe you didn't know that. You've never seen them?"

I shook my head and stood straight. Something had begun to

vibrate in the back of my mind, a need to see those sketches. I listened, and my astonishment grew.

“A few years after Faith adopted me,” he said, straightening and turning to lean back against the railing, “I came across the sketchbooks in the library. I asked her about them because I was so surprised to see them. I didn’t think anyone else could see the fae. Faith didn't know that they'd been drawn from life, she just thought it was a quirky collection started a few generations back that those with artistic skill in the family wanted to keep alive. That was when I told her that I could see fae. She believed me because she already knew by that time that I could see ghosts. Your aunt is aptly named,” he chuckled.

I stood frozen to the spot, my mouth open.

"Look at you. You're astonished," Jasher smiled and stepped closer.

I closed my mouth. "A little," I admitted. But I was *a lot* astonished.

"I can guess what you'll be doing this afternoon." He put his fingertips under my chin and tilted my face up to his. He dropped a soft kiss onto my lips. I kissed him back, but I was distracted by what he'd just told me. He pulled back and dropped his hand. "You'll find them in the old white cabinet, the one with the glass doors and brass knobs."

As we turned to step off the bridge, one of my flip flops caught on a rough patch of wood. My bare foot landed in the grass, leaving my flip flop behind. My foot suddenly felt as though roots had shot out of the bottom my sole and penetrated deep into the earth. The sensation halted my step, and I stumbled and fell. The attachment let go as quickly as it had come, and my foot sprang free from the ground.

"You alright?" Jasher put a hand under my arm to help me up.

I flushed, embarrassed. I covered it with a laugh, but I checked the sole of my foot uneasily. Nothing appeared to be amiss, there were no roots coming out of the bottom. Jasher picked up my shoe and handed it to me.

The sensation had scared me, but by the time we were entering the mudroom, I'd convinced myself that I had imagined it. I had just tripped on something.

After lunch, as Jasher was getting ready to go back to work, he asked, "Who did you see that was plagued by these demons, Georjie? Someone in town?" We were in the mudroom, Jasher was seated on the bench and pulling on his steel toed work boots.

"Yes. A man named Brendan. I actually met him on the first day..." I stopped when I saw his reaction. "What's wrong?"

Jasher had paused with one boot half done up. He looked up at me, and his face lost all color – a tricky thing for such a tanned man to pull off.

I put a hand on his shoulder. "Do you know him?"

"Aye." He bent to tie up the rest of his boot. "Aye, I know him." He stood and put his baseball cap on, pulling it down over his curls, face still pale. "Brendan is my da."

He left without another word. I covered my mouth with my hands, wishing that I had never told him what I had seen.

CHAPTER 21

The library in the Sheehan house has a feeling of political conversations long past, of readers once toasting their feet in front of the fireplace, with kerosene lamps or perhaps candles on side tables lighting their pages. Bookcases lined with volumes sit between each window as well as either side of the fireplace. Furniture that belongs in an antique store is clustered around the fireplace, and an old snooker table sits beneath an oil painting of my grandparents. A huge old bible sits on an antique wooden pulpit in the corner gathering an impressive layer of dust. A variety of black and white photographs, pressed flowers, framed newspaper clippings, and drawings grace the walls. The Sheehan family tree, drawn by hand probably a half-century ago, hangs over the fireplace.

I went straight to the bookcase Jasher had directed me to, and opened the glass cabinet doors. A long row of spines without titles faced me. The books were all different sizes, and colors, and some were in various states of decay. I chose a random spine, pulled it out, and opened it.

The first image I saw was of a fine-boned yellow faerie with gossamer wings. His limbs were curled over his body and he wore a sleepy expression. The image was beautifully rendered. It was clearly done in Jasher's hand. Every page was filled with a portrait of a freshly hatched faerie, their wings looking damp, their faces sleepy.

The sound of wind picked up and the light coming through the windows dimmed as clouds shifted to cover the sun. I put Jasher's sketchbook back and inspected the row. The books on the right side looked so old they were spotted and stained by dust, the spines were cracked and the edges frayed. I took another from the middle of the shelf.

My jaw went slack. It too was filled with portraits of fae, but done by a different artist. The inside cover was dated 1943. This artwork was done in watercolor, and the work was not as masterful as Jasher's. I flipped to the front of the book, searching for the name of the artist. The name Syracuse Sheehan was there, scratched in a messy scrawl. Syracuse was my great-grandad and had passed long before I'd been born. I replaced the book and took another, older one.

I opened it gingerly, and the pages were soft with age. The date on the inside cover was 1928. The artwork here was again different, and done by a monster talent. I flipped to the front page, looking for a name. It was there: Mailís Stiobhard. I'd never heard the name before. Her work was done in pencil only, no color had been added. The shading was so masterful and soft that it seemed early morning sunlight dusted the features of each fae. I took the sketchbook to the sofa near the fireplace and sat down with it open on my lap. I turned through each page, swept away by the beauty of the drawings. Goose-flesh crawled over my scalp. Unlike any of the other sketchbooks, each portrait had a name. Interesting. Why was this Mailís the only one who knew their names?

There were still more sketchbooks that looked older than this one. I opened them all. My wonder and amazement grew with each one. Each artist had their own particular style: pencil, pen and ink, watercolor, chalk. I pulled out the sketchbook farthest to the left, presumably the oldest as they'd been shelved chronologically, and opened it. The inside cover had the year 1867 scrawled in the top right corner.

When I turned to the first drawing in the oldest sketchbook, my dreams came rushing back to me with sudden and crystal clarity. They hit me with all the weight and velocity of a locomotive. My head snapped up and my eyes went wide. My vision blurred out of focus as I remembered, and I gasped.

I'm not sure how long I sat there, recalling the details of the dreams. It was as though that corner of my memory finally had a flashlight shone into it, I had to look around, casting the beam of light on every detail. When the initial shock of remembrance passed, and my vision finally came back to me, I looked more closely at the art.

My heart thudded when I saw the first painting. I flipped through a few more pages, just to be sure. It was these exact sketches I had seen in my dream. Outlined in black and filled in with colored ink, the images leapt from the page like light illuminated a stained glass window. The entire portrait had an elaborate border that reminded me of what I'd seen in very old bibles. These were the oldest sketches, but there were still no names written on these pages - and yet I knew the names anyway.

"Eda", I whispered as I looked at the familiar portrait. Her face seemed so alive. I turned the page but already knew what I would see. 'Po. I continued on. They were all there, and I knew all of them.

Tera. J'al. Mehda.

They were in the same order and exactly the way they'd appeared in my dreams.

"Oka. Iri. Bohe. Wenn." I said the last four names out loud, half expecting to feel a breeze, but there was no accompanying wind.

I looked up and scanned the mess of portraits and articles on the wall near the fireplace. My eye found what it was seeking: the family tree - rendered on parchment paper and framed. It was surrounded by a cluster of photographs. I recognized none of the faces on the wall save for my grandparents, who smiled out of a black and white wedding photograph - their cheeks round and soft with youth. Padraig and Roisin. Married in 1946. Aunt Faith hadn't come along until eighteen years later in 1964. Then Liz, in 1967. My grandmother had been forty. I looked for the name of the artist responsible for the drawings I held: Biddy. I found it. Her lifespan was marked as 1822-1892.

I wandered back to the sofa without looking at where I was going, sat, and consumed every drawing again. When I'd finally closed the last book, I didn't move for a very long time. The evidence was clear - my ancestors had been recording the fae for at least 150 years. Unless there were more sketchbooks that had been destroyed or were kept somewhere else, I had dreamed of the oldest fae.

Based on the variety of artistic styles, five different artists had each taken their turn building this...what could I call it?My eyes wandered back to the bookshelf, crammed with years of drawings. The word that came to mind was *archive*. That's what it was - an archive. Had the fae depicted in these books all hatched on this property? Probably. This house was two hundred years old. So, many of my ancestors had been able to see fae. It was Biddy's artwork I had dreamed about, but only one artist, Mailís, had written their names down. I had to deduce that was because she was the only one who could hear them. Just like I could.

I went back to the family tree and looked for her name. There - on the same line as Padraig and Niamh, my grandfather and his twin sister. But the line with her name extended off to the side, almost like she was an afterthought. Mailís Stiobhard-Sheehan. 1903 - 1935. Why such a short life? She was a much older half-sister to my grandfather - same mother, different father.

In a bottom corner of the collection cramming the wall, my eyes were arrested by a pencil drawing of a dark-haired woman in a chevron patterned dress. She was sitting in a chair by a fireplace. I looked over at the fire corner in the far wall, noting the flourish in the center of the wooden mantle. It was the same mantle in the drawing.

The woman's eyes were soft and dark and her expression neither a frown nor a smile. Her eyes seemed to cling to mine no matter where I stood. I peered closer and blew the film of dust from the glass. Her hair had a severe part down the middle and was tied low at the nape of her neck. She had the same bump on the bridge of her nose as my grandfather, Padraig. I put a finger to my nose. I had the same rise on the bridge of my nose too, albeit smaller, I hoped. I pulled the small frame off the wall and turned it over. Someone had written on the back: *Mailís Stiobhard-Sheehan. Self-Portrait. 1929.* She'd died only a mere six years after she'd done this self-portrait.

Each artist, except for Jasher, had been a blood relative. But Jasher could see ghosts. Now, for some reason I didn't understand, I could see the fae, too. A chill swept through me and I pulled my cardigan closed. It couldn't have been a dream. No dream could be that accurate. It was impossible.

My phone chirped and I jumped with a loud gasp. My heart bolted like a sprinter. I grabbed my phone from the coffee table.

Saxony: *What are you doing?*

Me: *Getting lost in family history. Apparently, there is a lot of artistic talent in my family.*

Saxony: *Huh, too bad it skipped your generation.*

I snorted a laugh. She was right, I couldn't draw stick people. *Brat,* I texted back. *What are you doing?*

Saxony: *I... have a date with a very cute Italian man. Don't wait up.*

Me: *Which one is this?*

Saxony had already told me that she'd met two guys, both cute, both charming.

Saxony: *Dante.*

Me: *The glass-blower?*

I waited, but she didn't reply. I put my phone back. She'd probably text me in the middle of the night.

By this time, the library was a mess of open sketchbooks scattered on the couch and coffee table, and I was genuinely spooked. I needed answers, and I felt instinctively that they lay with Mailís.

I became a sleuth, and raided the library shelves in search of anything that might contain answers. My grandparents had both journaled, it was something their mother passed down to them. Maybe Mailís had journaled too. Half a dozen paper cuts later, and with filthy black fingers, I struck gold. A small black book hidden amongst a stack of others just like it. Diaries and memoirs.

The title page was handwritten in a delicate cursive. Ink splatters misted over the fine wispy letters: *Mailís Stiobhard.* I was so excited to find it, and so relieved that it was in English and not Gaelic, that I kissed it.

CHAPTER 22

The wind outside had picked up, and rain blurred the glass. I hurriedly put the library back together, arranging the journals and sketchbooks as best I could before heading downstairs and making myself some tea. I scooched into the kitchen nook with my find as the rain pattered down outside, and began to read.

It wasn't really a diary, more of an artists' study. The pages were filled with drawings of people and animals. Her skill with a pencil was good. Even though the sketches were mostly doodles, they were a pleasure to look at. The face of a middle-aged woman wearing a bonnet bent over beside a wood stove with kindling in her hands. The door of the stove was open and the firelight was so well rendered on her face and clothing that I could almost hear the crackling flames. 'Mama' was scribbled under the drawing.

She also had drawings of a puppy, the eyes and eyelashes of a cow, the mouth of a cow with the tongue licking up into its nose. Mailís missed no detail - the hair, the glistening saliva, the taste buds on the tongue.

I passed more drawings of people, some named, some not. Many were just studies of hands, eyes, lips. I stopped at a completed portrait of a man from the chest up. His dark hair curled from under his cap, and a scarf was knotted at his throat. He wasn't smiling, but somehow she'd captured that he was happy just the same. There were hardly any fine lines indicating age, just a few along the forehead and lining the mouth. She'd scrawled 'Da' below the drawing. Whatever had happened to Mailís, one thing was for certain, she was talented, and her skill transitioned from good to extraordinary. Flipping through these pages was like watching years of artistic growth in fast-motion.

She experimented with different techniques: using circular scribbles to render an image of a landscape, crosshatching a portrait of a fresh young woman named Irene, even a watercolor of a robin in the grass - the first colored image. After this painting was the first written entry of substance. The hair on my arms stood at attention as I read the first line. It felt as though it had been written just for me.

Last night I had the strangest dream, and it wasn't the first of its kind.

The hair at the nape of my neck stood on end. Then I couldn't read fast enough.

It's taken me a long time to remember, but now that I have, they're as clear as a cloudless day. I dreamed of drifting through a wet fog. I could feel nothing beneath my feet, I floated - like a ghost. I came to a bookshelf full of sketchbooks, and pulled one from the shelf. It was full of drawings of faeries. In my dream, I knew the names and said them out loud, one after the other. I feel ridiculous when I think of how much I believed in faeries in my dream. They seemed quite real to me.

My heart pounded under my ribs, rattling against my sternum like it was trying to escape.

Every time I called a name, I felt a warm wind. There was the sound of an exhale while I inhaled, as I took the faerie breath in. It smelled of moss and living things. With each inhale, I sank lower and lower, until my feet were flat on the earth.

My hand flew to my mouth. According to Mailís, we had breathed in the exhales of the fae. And, what? We'd taken in their power? I lay the book face down on the table. I needed a moment to process. No, I needed a lifetime to process. My palms were cold and clammy and the skin between my breasts felt damp. I couldn't handle this. This was...

crazy. I stared at the ceiling and put my cold palm over my heart, willing it to slow.

With trembling fingers, I picked up the diary again and turned the page. There it was - the drawing of a faerie. The first one Mailís ever rendered. At the top of the page were the words: *I understand.*

"What do you understand, Mailís? I said out loud. "You understand why there were sketchbooks full of faeries in your library? Or something bigger?" I turned the page.

From that point on, the sketches of people and animals disappeared. What took their place were drawings of fae, all of them looking freshly hatched. Then the sketches of plants began to appear - detailed to the point of botanical studies. The sketches of plants often included scribbled notes and old-world Gaelic names.

Whatever was happening to me, it had happened to Mailís first. My fear began to dissolve, and gratitude for Mailís filled its place. I turned the page over to a handwritten entry. It was the longest by far of any of her written passages, and it hit home like an arrow in the bullseye of my heart.

Something is happening to me. I can feel things that I never felt before. I know things that I never knew before. I don't know where this knowledge is coming from. I can only connect it to the fae, and my dreams. I discovered a plant that I had never known growing near the spring, a scented herb named Lus na Cnámh Briste. It introduced itself to me when I touched it. Through the pads of my fingers I knew that this plant had healing properties.

I was also introduced to Fraochán, a berry which told me that it could be consumed to strengthen the thin membrane surrounding the human brain and bring resilience to the skin. The moment I came into contact with it, I understood it. I am having some difficulty in making a decision about this knowledge which I have acquired. It is no secret that I am already regarded as a wistful and reclusive spinster, preferring the company of nature to that of people. For now I shall keep it to myself and these pages.

Her mental musings stopped there and the drawings commenced again. It was several pages later before there were words again, and they made me stop.

Today, I healed myself of a painful headache. I knew that cohosh was good for such a thing. I went to gather some to make a tincture, but when I touched it, the world of the herb was given to me. I was able to draw the healing energy into myself, I could feel my headache ease, more rapidly than it would have if I had taken the tincture. I am becoming a Wise. I have been chosen by the fae. I am ashamed that I did not believe.

A Wise. The term echoed and vibrated. Wise was what the fae had said to me the night they hatched, but it hadn't made any sense to me. Now it did. Wise wasn't an adjective, it was a who.

"What's a Wise, Mailís?" I whispered. I turned the page to find more botanical drawings, more studies of fae - their tiny hands, their transparency and ethereal light. I skipped past the drawings, used to them by now. I needed more information.

I stopped at the next block of writing but was frustrated when her entry changed subjects entirely.

Cousin Irene has forced me to attend the Ana Christmas dance, and never was I more grateful for being dragged somewhere against my will. I have met the most genteel soul. Irene's friend Eoin introduced his brother to our party, a singular Cormac O'Brien.

I paused. O'Brien? Why was that name familiar?

I read on. Over the next several entries, Mailís wrote about the fear of her own feelings as she met with Cormac on public outings. It was easy to gather that Mailís was not used to socializing but that she pushed herself out of her comfort zone, solely for the young man's company. Several cryptic phrases had been scrawled amidst drawings of plants and fae. Until finally... the clincher:

I am in love.

My heart melted for her. This woman, whose existence was completely unknown to me before the summer, had suddenly come to mean so much to me. And her happiness was my happiness. Those four simple words made my heart feel as light as a balloon, and eased the gnawing curiosity, if only for a moment.

I turned over another page and gasped when I saw a black and white pencil portrait of a young man, unlabeled. This was almost undoubtedly Cormac O'Brien. I wondered if she'd drawn it from memory, or from life. His hair was combed forward in the fashion of the day, and curled in front of his ears. He wore a high collar, standing up nearly to his strong square jawline. His hair was dark, and may have been black. He had high cheekbones, a high aristocratic forehead, and full sensual lips with a tiny scar on the upper lip.

"Oh Mailís," I breathed as I took in the dark eyes, the ever so slightly arrogant tilt of the chin, the aquiline nose. She'd captured the masculine beauty of his face, but also his spirit. He was aloof, proud, and I couldn't say for sure because it could have just been the effect of the scar, but I thought his lip curled with a touch of cruelty. My mind flashed back to the self-portrait in the library of Mailís in her chevron dress, with her soft, vulnerable eyes. "He's so wrong for you."

CHAPTER 23

The next morning found me moving about in a daze. I had taken the diary to bed with me after supper so I could continue reading and looking through the sketches, but I had quickly fallen asleep. Exhausted from all the revelation, I suspect.

I slept in past eight and woke to more rain on the windows. I turned on the gas stove and set the kettle over it to boil. I pulled down the jar of Irish breakfast tea and set two bags in the teapot. The back door opened and Jasher came in, scraping his boots on the mat.

"Georjie? That you?"

"I'm here. Morning. Forget something?"

"Aye, a parka," he laughed. "If you go out today, take your rain jacket. It's cold and wet. You'd think it was March."

I looked out the window at the gray skies and drizzle, then poked my head into the mudroom. Jasher was zipping up an oilskin coat.

"How are you working in this awful weather?" I asked.

"Most of it is indoors. All I have to do that's outside is measure." He grabbed his baseball cap and jammed it on his head. "Still reading that diary?"

"Yes. Sorry I'm neglecting you. It's fascinating."

He smiled. "We're like an old married couple by now."

The kettle began to whistle behind me. "Speaking of which," I took on the croaky, dry tone of an old withered woman. "Want to take some hot tea with you, my dear?"

He laughed. "You should have been an actress. I would love some. But only if it's ready now, I'm running late. We're meeting at the yard to make an order."

"You got it. Stay there, I'll bring it to you. Two seconds." I found a tall slender aluminum thermos in the cupboard, rinsed it with hot water and pushed two teabags in through the narrow mouth. I turned off the burner and filled the thermos and the teapot with boiling water. "Milk?"

"Just a splash!" Jasher yelled from the mudroom. "Thanks, Georjie. You're a goddess!"

I smiled, snatched the milk from the fridge and poured a dash into the thermos. I spun away from the thermos with the milk in my hand and hit it, knocking it over. Boiled water splashed down the front of my right thigh and the back of my right wrist. A cry of pain ripped from my throat and I dropped the milk. Tears sprang to my eyes as the hot water scorched my skin. I doubled over and clenched my teeth. It was the kind of burn that makes your whole body stiffen up and the nerves scream for mercy.

"Georjie!" Jasher ran into the room in his boots, leaving a trail of muck. "Bloody hell! What happened?" I felt his hand on my lower back. "Are you all right?"

I stood and cranked on the cold water. "Burned myself." I soaked a dishrag in cold water and pressed it to my thigh, and held my wrist under the running water. The heat eased, but the searing pain was still there. I squeezed my eyes shut.

"You scared the bejaysus out of me. I didn't need tea that bad. Here." He opened the cupboard and pulled down a tin with a piece of masking tape stuck to the lid. On the tape, Faith's fine scrawl read 'Lavender Salve.' He spun open the lid. "Put this on. It works."

"Thanks, you'd better go. Sorry about the tea." I forced a pain-filled smile at him. "I got it." I wanted to examine my thigh but I wasn't about to take my pants down in front of Jasher.

"Don't worry about that. You're sure you're alright? Do you need a doctor?" Jasher's eyes bounced between my wet leg and my face. A line had appeared between his eyes.

Visions of men in white coats with needles loomed in my imagination. "No, it's not that bad. It'll smart for a few days, but I'll be fine. Go on."

"I hate to leave you like this."

His concern already made me feel a bit better. "I'll be alright. I'm a big girl. Go on, Jasher. I'll see you later."

He nodded and gave my shoulder a squeeze. He clomped toward the door. "Uh..." he looked down at the muddy footprints.

"I'll clean up, don't worry."

"Sorry," he said with a wince. He disappeared into the mudroom and I heard the back door open. "Use the salve!" he called, and the door slammed.

"Right." I blew a strand of hair away from my face and turned off the cold water. I looked at the back of my wrist. The skin was red and raw, the pain still intense. My hand trembled. My thigh felt like someone had held the side of a red-hot knife to it. I reached for the tin of salve when my eyes fell on the lavender plant sitting on the breakfast table in the nook.

...when I touched it, the world of the herb was given to me...

I limped over to the table and looked down at it. Lavandula Dentata. I bent to smell the fragrant leaves, sighing with pleasure. I reached out a tentative finger and touched a leaf.

The plant lit up with a fine misty green glow, and I gasped. A thread of light wound through every leaf and stem. The healing qualities of the plant filled my mind and an energy thrummed through my fingers, making every nerve tingle. It traveled right down to the soles of my feet. A hunger for what the plant contained clutched at my guts. I was famished, needy. I drew on the energy, feeling the chemical compounds multiply exponentially as they traveled through my cells. The nerves in my hand buzzed like bees. The buzzing traveled through my wrist, up my arm, and into my spine and chest. When it hit my heart I could feel it sweep out through every vein.

All sensation of heat and pain vanished. I took my finger away from the plant and stood there, panting. The light of the plant faded and the buzzing energy subsided, leaving behind a pleasurable throb of vitality.

I put a hand over my heart, feeling its rapid beat. I laughed and then hiccupped. "I think you're my new favorite plant," I said to the lavender.

I looked at the skin of my wrist. It was as though the burn had never happened. There was no pain anymore. Nothing. The only evidence that I'd spilled tea was the wet stain on my pants. I fell into a chair. My breathing slowed. I looked at the lavender, sitting there benignly in its pot. It had given everything to me but remained unchanged.

But I...

I was very, very changed. I grabbed the diary and opened to where I'd left off the evening before.

CHAPTER 24

It was the term *earth elemental* that did the most to answer my question of what a Wise was, but it was the word 'residual' that made me go out in the rain.

I am astounded with this new power. With a simple handful of soil, I am able to see a residual of past events, almost as though I were present in history. All I need do is ask the soil to show me with a thought. It seems these residuals are left behind when events have been left unfinished, and a Wise (earth elemental?), has access to them.

After I read that, everything grew quiet and I sat back, thoughtful. An earth elemental. The rain poured, pattering against the windowpanes. I may as well have had cotton stuffed in my ears for all that I paid attention to it.

I set the diary on the table and got up. Mailís was a Wise, I was a Wise. I should be able to do what she had described. I didn't bother pulling on a rain jacket. I opened the door and stepped outside. I walked down the stone path and onto the grass, my wet feet already sliding on my flip-flops. I felt neither cold nor hot, excited nor trepidatious. I had gone very quiet inside.

I crossed the lawn and went to the garden where the earth was softest, and stood there looking down at the black soil. Closing my eyes, I thought of Mailís. Then I crouched and plunged my fingers into the garden, muck wedging under my fingernails. I stood, with the lump of earth in my palm. I scanned the backyard, and when the residual images of Mailís and Cormac appeared, I took a shallow breath and stepped back.

They looked like figures on a television with bad reception; thin lines of disruption and pixelation blurred their edges. I was learning that a Wise was someone who knew nature like it was part of them, was able to draw the healing power of the earth into themselves, and now...

Mailís had written that residuals were left behind when events had been left unresolved and they play over and over in perpetuity on a loop. A Wise can see them, if she chooses. And there they were, their shapes had risen from the ground. Not ghosts, but a simple imprint left behind by human energy. They had no consciousness, they couldn't hear or see me, they had no ability to respond. Just old energy stuck in replay.

Mailís wore the chevron dress that I had come to associate with her. She was taller than I'd imagined, with long slender limbs and hands. She walked across the back of the yard, and at her side was the figure of a tall man with dark curly hair and broad shoulders. Cormac. They were talking, but the residual had no audio. I had to guess from their facial expressions and body language the topic of their discussion. They were walking close together, shoulder to shoulder, but not touching. Mailís's shoulders were turned slightly toward Cormac and she was speaking with her hands. His head was inclined toward her, engrossed by her. I felt disconnected from my body as I watched the residuals cross the lawn and step up onto the small bridge.

They stopped there, talking. They loved one another, that was clear. It was when they bent to lean their elbows on the railing of the bridge, that my heart began to pound. My fist closed around the soil in my hand and squeezed. They looked just like Jasher and I would have looked to an outsider only the day before. We had stood on the bridge and talked just like that, we had leaned with our elbows on the railing, just like them. To anyone who may have been watching, we would have looked identical to the residual that was in front of me now. I watched them until they turned toward each other and Cormac stepped closer to her, his arm snaking around her waist. He put a tender finger under her chin and tilted her face up. Maybe he had loved her? Maybe I was wrong about the conclusion I had jumped to when I saw his portrait. He leaned down, canting his head to the side. Mailís tilted her face up to be kissed, and closed her eyes.

I dropped the soil, feeling like a voyeur, and the residual disappeared. I let the rain wash away the dirt on my hand as I stood there and processed the vision.

I returned to the house. I took a break from reading the diary only long enough to shower and change. My mind was a whirlwind. It was good that Jasher had to work, and that Faith was away. I was in a sort of intellectual shock and needed time to absorb. My hands were steady as I toweled off and dressed in jeans and a cotton hoodie. I pulled on a thick pair of socks and tied my hair back as I went down the stairs. There, I snatched the diary off the counter and slid into the kitchen nook again.

I am not one for wishing to go back and change the past, what's done is done. But oh how I could have benefited from more time with my grandfather before he passed on.

I looked up, wracked my brains for the name, came up empty. I picked up my phone and opened the photo of the family tree I had taken, just to help with my memory. Liam Stiobhard - one of the artists.

All I can recall is that a Wise is someone the ancient fae have gifted with the power to know nature intimately, and draw from it, in some cases to control it, although I've no idea how. This knowledge that I am acquiring is growing daily, but so far is limited to touch. How strong will these abilities become?

My eyes skimmed over the next several entries, which were not about her powers, but about her falling in love with Cormac O'Brien. Weeks passed by without entry, then a random sketch of a plant would appear, always one with powerful effects on the human body. Finally, an entry professing her love for Cormac.

Our passion seems boundless. At an age when most women are looking forward to grandchildren, God has finally seen fit to bless me.

Mailís was only 31 when she wrote those words. You've got to have a little appreciation for how times have changed. Nowadays if a woman isn't married at 31, nobody so much as blinks.

...I have finally met my love. My match. I feel deep in my bones how much he loves me. The way I can read a plant with my fingertips, I can feel the authenticity of his love when I hold his hand. And oh, how I love him, too. My Cormac.

"How sweet, Mailís," I said. I flipped past several more sketches, skimming the words.

These are the happiest days of my life. We are engaged. When all hope was long lost that I would ever have a family of my own, sweet Cormac appears: a gift from God. I know there are young ladies in town who've been thwarted by our love. Young Miss Ó Súilleabháin, so called 'Aileen the Flirt' by Irene, still makes me uncomfortable in how she makes eyes at my Cormac, but God has shown he knows better. Now my only hope is that God finds in his heart enough generosity for me that I might bear children at so advanced an age.

I flipped past more drawings. "Whoa," I said as I turned the page. The handwriting of this entry looked so different from the rest. Harder.

I am betrayed. If the powers of a Wise lead her into deception, then why should anyone want such a blessing? Cormac has given a child to another, even before they are wed. Oh, how Ana will laugh. What good is all of my wisdom, when I am so utterly and terribly broken.

"Oh no," I whispered. My vision blurred at the heartbreak pouring onto the page. She'd been cheated on by the only man she'd ever loved. She thought her life was saved, but instead, he'd stabbed her in the heart. *He has given a child to another.*

The next few pages were empty. I flipped forward. "No," I breathed. That was it? No more about becoming a Wise? "No, no, no..." I peeled through the pages, but there was nothing. Something yellow caught my eye as I flipped and I went back. It was an article shoved into the book, an old newspaper clipping. After reading it, it was clear that it had not been put there by Mailís's hand.

4 March 1935. MISSING, Woman, aged 32, standing at 5 feet, 8 inches, fair of skin, slender build, grey eyes, black hair parted down the middle; seen wearing a black high-collared dress, felt hat, and brown leather shoes. Last seen walking down Molesly Street, Anacullough at midday on Thursday last. Information leading to discovery shall be handsomely rewarded. Apply to 4 Ballinlough St, Anacullough, EIRE.

Isn't it funny how a partial answer just spawns more questions? There was nothing after this. Jasher wasn't home, Faith was gone, the house was quiet, and yet the silence after reading that clipping was deafening.

I got up and took the stairs two and a time to the library. After spending another hour there, tearing through the same old journals, combing the walls and reading anything that looked like it came out of an old newspaper, I was beyond frustrated. I tucked the diary and the clipping into a bag, eyeballed the rain, which didn't seem to be slowing, grabbed my rain jacket from the mudroom, and biked into town.

CHAPTER 25

The library in Ana was an ancient construction compared to the library in Saltford, and the librarian looked as though she'd worked there since the day the stone building had been erected. At least she still had her own teeth, and displayed them frequently in a smile. Dressed in a tweed skirt and vest with a creamy blouse and billowy sleeves, she looked like a character in an old movie.

I peeled off my wet rain jacket and hung it on the coat rack inside the door. Shelves of books surrounded long tables equipped with green glass lamps. Three elderly men sat scattered along the tables, each absorbed in study. The librarian sat behind an oak desk that looked like it weighed more than a half-ton truck. I wiped my face with my sleeve and crossed the rippling wooden floor. I pulled the diary out of my bag.

The name "Mrs. McMurtry" was written on a name-plate that faced outward on the desk. Her thin gray hair had been pulled up into a bun and a half dozen silver barrettes held everything in place. She looked up and smiled and a thousand wrinkles sprang to life as her kindly eyes took me in.

"What can I do for you, Miss?" she said so quietly it was almost a whisper. She recognized me, I'd been in the library before, but this was the first time we'd spoken.

"I was wondering if you kept records of old newspapers?"

"Of course."

"I'm trying to find out what happened to an ancestor of mine." I opened the diary to the page where the clipping was taped and showed it to her.

She took it with arthritic fingers and held it low in front of her. She tilted her head to read it through her bifocals. Her mouth moved silently as she read the clipping's contents. She gave me a sympathetic look and handed it back to me. "We might be able to help you," she said, slowly, thinking. "All of our microfilm is on the second floor. You can search the index by surname, that ought to turn something up."

I followed her up the wide staircase and into a dark room with only two small pools of light from floor lamps. The room was a good ten degrees hotter than the first floor and sweat dampened my upper lip and forehead.

The librarian led me into an alcove with three clunky looking metal jalopies with large square screens. They had to be from the sixties. "These are the readers. They're a little finicky so be gentle with them. We have new ones on order but they aren't due for another month. I'll show you where we store the microfilm."

We passed through a set of double doors. She touched a switch beside the door and anemic fluorescent lighting flickered to life. Yards and yards of metal bureaus stretched out before us. I began to sweat in earnest, and not just from the heat.

"Here is our microfilm storage," she began. She must have caught the look of panic on my face because she followed up with, "Don't worry, dear. We have more than one way of categorizing things. When looking for the result of a missing persons case, it might be easiest to start at the death indexes. What name was it?"

Why hadn't I thought of that? This ancient well-dressed librarian had been down this road before. "Sheehan."

"Okay, and what year was the disappearance, again?" She tilted her head down toward the diary where I'd stowed the clipping away, but I knew it from memory by now.

"1935. In March."

"Good." She beelined for a particular aisle. "Take heart, Miss. You've got more factual information to start with than most people who come in here looking for answers." She skimmed over the typed face-cards on the fronts of the drawers. "Some poor souls spend years in here," she mumbled, "searching for a needle in a stack of needles, going on nothing but a wing and a prayer. Here we are." She laid a hand on the top of the metal shelves. "Here are the death indexes beginning in January of 1935. Time ascends this way," she sliced a hand back toward the door. "And everything is alphabetical. If your ancestor turned up dead, you'll be able to find her name in the death notices or obits sometime after March 1935. Do you know how to use the micro-reader?"

I nodded. "I think so." They couldn't be much different than the ones we had in our school library. I thanked her and she left me to it.

I won't bore you with the searching part - it's enough to say that my eyes skimmed a whole lot of obituaries over the hour and a half it took me to find her. I had a bad moment when I remembered that Mailís wouldn't have been registered as a Sheehan, but a Stiobhard-Sheehan. I had to start over, focusing on the St's not the Sh's. Let me tell you I uttered more than one 'sh' word. It might make a better story to say that I didn't eat for days, and I endured a sore back and a wrist injury as I combed the vaults of history, but actually, thanks to the fine organization of the staff at the Ana County Library, I found her in less than two hours.

6 April 1937 *Missing Persons Case Unofficially Ruled Suicide.*

Two years after the disappearance of Miss Mailís Stiobhard-Sheehan, which has flummoxed the Garda, the case remains unsolved, the Sheehan family unsatisfied. "Miss Stiobhard-Sheehan experienced personal tragedy shortly before her disappearance," stated Police Inspector Murray Ó Cuinn. "Due to several character reports of Miss Stiobhard's emotional instability, it is our strong belief that she is most likely a suicide. Though we cannot offi-

cially mark the case as closed without producing material evidence, we motion to lay the investigation to rest. We've done all that could be done for her and her family. May Miss Stiobhard-Sheehan rest in peace." Family members have declined to comment beyond requesting privacy.

I felt like I'd been kicked in the teeth. More than two years after she'd disappeared, they'd finally given up. Personal tragedy. Suicide. My heart broke for her. She'd been so excited and in love. It was worse than Romeo and Juliet, because at least they ended up together in the end, even if it was in death. Poor Mailís was dead and alone.

A fuzzy black and white photograph of a woman accompanied the article. The image had no caption. The clarity was poor, and half the woman's face and all of her hair were concealed under a bonnet. It was the bump on the bridge of her nose that gave her away.

I sat back in my chair, chin in hand, for I don't know how long. The residual I had seen didn't come with a caption announcing the date, but Mailís's diary was pretty clear. The last entry had come shortly before she'd been reported missing. It was more than unsettling, it was disturbing, not the least of which was my connection to her. She'd become a Wise, I was becoming a Wise. I'd walked the bridge with Jasher, and he'd kissed me. She'd walked the bridge with Cormac, and he'd kissed her. She disappeared. And I... I was still here, for now.

She had been excited about life, about to get married, was madly in love, had been gifted by the fae. Had the papers gotten it wrong and she'd transformed fully into whatever it was she (and I) were becoming? They'd never found a body. Maybe she had morphed into a faerie and disappeared into the earth? I sighed, not really believing that. It didn't look good.

Nausea clenched at my stomach. On the outside, becoming a Wise seemed like a blessing - the ability to capture the healing forces of nature and channel them is pretty spectacular. But where did it end? Revelations had been happening regularly and frequently, each one more astounding than the last. I was on a runaway horse without bit or bridle. When and where he stopped was anyone's guess.

My fingers had grown cold, and my heart felt small and wrung out. By the time I thanked the librarian for her help and found my way to my bike, I was sick with fear. Toward what kind of fate was I barreling?

CHAPTER 26

The rain had finally stopped by the time I left the library. Everything was wet and dripping. I wiped off the bike seat, threw a leg over, and headed in the direction of Sarasborne.

My stomach grumbled, and my eyes felt heavy. My mind continued to roll around the possibilities that these things happening to me would continue to grow and change. The idea that Mailís had taken her own life was mind-boggling.

As I pedaled, I realized I'd missed the turn-off for the bike path to the house. Shrugging, I took the road instead. The cool wind rustled the leaves of the oaks lining the road, and whipped my hair into my mouth. I picked up the pace, eyeballing the gathering clouds on the horizon. The rain wasn't over, this was just an intermission. Just time enough to buy popcorn and licorice before the show started again. A flash of light flickered several times in the undersides of faraway clouds. The last hill before our driveway was within sight, so I stood and bore down on the pedals to get speed.

What is it they say about most accidents happening close to home? It certainly rang true for me that day. I was cresting that last hill when a farm truck going in the opposite direction (driving like he was an emergency vehicle on a mission instead of a rickety rig hauling a load of sheep) loomed abruptly, materializing from wisps of fog. The sight of the truck snapped me back into the present so hard I got mental whiplash. My scream was echoed by his horn blast as I swerved toward the ditch. The wind from his passing whipped my clothes and every loose particle of dirt on that road blew into my eyes. The bike wobbled and I knew I was going to fall - funny how that moment of realization is more terrifying than the actual event. I fought to keep my eyes open but they were so grit-filled that it was simply impossible. The handlebars turned, the front wheel slammed sideways, and over the bars I flew, landing in the mud in a tangle of limbs and metal. I skidded painfully along the gravel, sacrificing several inches of skin in the process.

The driver of the truck yelled something in Gaelic but didn't stop. I lay there on my stomach, eyes stinging and watering. The right side of my jaw, my forearm, my right knee, and both palms burned like someone was holding a lighter to my skin. I'm not sure how long I lay there before I dragged myself upright. "Bloody hell," I swore. Okay, maybe my cursing was a little worse than that. It took me several minutes to get myself back on my feet, brushed off, and limping home. The entire right side of my body ached, and my abrasions stung. Adrenalin had flooded my body and made my legs feel weak and my hands shake. The pain sucked, as it always does. I won't go on about it, just know that there was blood. Maybe I had to bleed before I could learn what I had to learn, and isn't that always the way?

I couldn't tell if I was more upset over Mailís's supposed suicide, or my fall, but it was the vegetation that cleared my head and made way for the residual I was about to see. As I passed a cluster of plants in the ditch, their healing properties clarified in my mind. Feeling compelled by some otherworldly power, I reached my fingers out and touched the leaves. Immediately, my mind was flooded with knowledge. Arnica had the power to diminish inflammation and bruising, and comfrey would knit together not only broken skin but also bones. The vegetation hummed under my fingertips and I could no more stop myself from drawing in their power than I could have prevented my fall. The nutrients within each plant condensed and entered my bloodstream, compounding many times over.

I say it was easy, but that isn't giving you the true sensation. It was a very strange feeling - a bit like trying to suck a thick gel through a straw. But as I sucked, my body filled with a beautiful energy, and it felt as though my cells and my blood were dancing. The pain of my wounds and the throbbing of my bruises faded. I looked down at my arm, watching the torn skin stitch back together as though by unseen needle and thread. Small stones were expelled as the wound mended and closed itself. A sprinkling of dirt and bits of gravel fell into the grass.

Understanding that the root of the plant was one of the most powerful parts, and under the impression that I needed to touch it, I knelt and began to dig, eager to see if the beautiful feeling changed or increased when my hands got tangled in the root. Mailís had written about the supercharged power of roots.

As my fingers raked the soil and clumps of earth filled my palms, I was startled by movement in my periphery. There was no sound to warn me, and so you can imagine what it did to my heart to look up and see the ghostly forms of two people having an argument at the end of the Sarasborne driveway. It took me a moment to recognize Mailís because I was beginning to know her by her chevron dress, but here she was wearing a solid dress in a dark color. The images in a residual come in black and white, so maybe her dress was navy, or brown, but to my eyes it appeared black. She had a high-necked collar with a ring of lace at the top, and a ruffle on her chest in the shape of a V. I was so startled that it took me several moments to register what I was seeing. Mailís and Cormac were having some kind of confrontation, and speaking with great passion. It was like watching a silent movie - dramatic, overstated, only this had far more authenticity than any film I'd ever seen.

I became a statue as I watched the scene play out before me - a still of a girl digging in the dirt in the ditch alongside the road. I came alive only when a residual horse came barreling into the scene from behind me and shocked me into movement. A man I didn't recognize rode into view on a workhorse with no saddle and a bridle made of rope. The man wore a dark jacket, and a black hat that hid his face. Everything about him spelled urgency. He pulled the horse up to where Cormac and Mailís stood. The animal tossed its head and reared low. The way the man was hunched made me realize it was raining the day this took place, and when I looked closer at Mailís and Cormac, I saw their hair was curly and damp, their skin shiny with wetness.

The man on horseback spoke to Cormac, who listened, with an arm held out toward Mailís. She had a hand hooked around his elbow and her eyes were wide and frightened. As they listened to the rider, Cormac's face hardened and Mailís began to cry. She was shaking her head, even as Cormac used the rider's arm to swing up behind him. As the horse wheeled, hoofs throwing clumps of dirt, Mailís collapsed to her knees. Neither of the men looked back as the horse galloped back the way it had come and disappeared from my view.

Mailís covered her face with her hands and bent her forehead to the earth. As she splayed her hands out on the ground in front of her and her fingers curled into the mud, displaying an agony that even her face could not rival, the residual blinked out and the figures of Cormac and Mailís appeared once again. The scene began anew and I saw the beginning that I had missed.

Cormac's face was away from me but it was clear the two were talking. As the conversation progressed, Mailís became more and more upset, shaking her head, her mouth pulled down. By the time the horseman appeared again, she was a piteous creature.

I felt wrecked. I watched the residual a half-dozen times, tears streaming down my own face, hands still in the dirt. It wasn't difficult to make some sense of what I was seeing. Cormac had broken Mailís's heart, just like I had thought he might. He left her literally in the mud, weeping and broken and alone. What their words were to one another, and what news the rider came to deliver I couldn't tell, but her agony was as clear as a full moon on a cloudless night. I didn't know how long she lay there after he left her because the residual reset itself before she got up, but a big piece of the puzzle had found its way to me.

Why did Cormac break Mailís's heart? He'd had such love on his face, that day they kissed on the bridge. My mind only had a single, feeble clue - and that was the name of the girl in the diary. Aileen the Flirt.

By the time I got to my feet and dusted my hands of soil, I had made up my mind to go back into town. I had another question to ask the librarian now. The residual faded away as the earth left my palms, and I mounted the bike, wheeled it around, and went back in the same direction the residual horse had carried Cormac and the other rider - back to Anacullough.

CHAPTER 27

If the librarian was surprised by my reappearance so shortly after I'd departed, she didn't show it. What a pro. I walked up to her desk, hair disheveled, hands still dirty from digging around in the ditch, fingernails black.

"Are you alright?" She gave my grubby appearance a cursory once over. She had neither alarm nor judgement in her expression. I suppose when you get to a certain age, it takes more than filthy hands to elicit a reaction.

"Apparently, I'm not finished," I said. "This time, I need the wedding indexes." I was physically tired and emotionally exhausted, but the need to know had sunk its hooks deep. There was no way I was going to stop now, not when my own fate might be tied to it.

"I see." She took off her bifocals and propped them on her head. She got up and circled the desk. I followed her toward the stairs. "Whose wedding are we after?"

"Aileen O'Sullivan. That would be the anglicized way to say it. I'm sorry I don't know how to pronounce it the Gaelic way." My hands were shaking as I grabbed the banister, whether from hunger or shock, I didn't know. Probably both.

The librarian halted on the stairs and swung back to me, her mouth in an 'O'. "Ó Súilleabháin?" she said. "When would this wedding have taken place?"

I frowned, thinking. "1935?"

"My dear," she put a withered hand on my shoulder. "Aileen Ó Súilleabháin is still alive. She's as ancient as the hills, but for mental stamina she'd put any college kid to shame. If it's the story you want, there won't be a better source than the horse's mouth, so to speak. She lives at the pensioners home and they're open for visitors all day most days."

I felt the blood drain from my face. I opened my mouth to protest but I didn't know what to say first. That it was impossible that it was the same Aileen, that I wouldn't know what to say to her, that I didn't feel right disturbing an old lady's peace, that I might strangle her if she admitted to stealing Cormac away from Mailís. Mailís's anguished face rose to my mind, her body as it collapsed like a puppet whose strings had been cut, her hooked fingers dragging in the dirt of the road.

"Go on, dear. I don't know her well, but I know she's a kind lady. It would probably make her day to have a visit from a curious lass such as yourself. Besides," she looked at her watch, "we're closing up soon. Sunny Valley is only three blocks east of here."

I found myself escorted brusquely but somehow kindly through the foyer and to the front doors. By the time I found my voice, I was standing outside and facing the right direction. "Sunny Valley has a public washroom just inside the front doors," the librarian added. "Maybe just a quick wash-up before you go to say hello." And with that, she disappeared back inside and I found myself closing the distance between me and one of Mailís's contemporaries.

I left my bike in the bike rack and went on foot, which allowed me to cut down a pedestrian walkway that bikes weren't allowed on. A pattering of rain had begun again. I pulled my hood up over my head and bent against the raindrops.

Sunny Valley was a low yellow brick building with a wheelchair-friendly ramp leading up to the door. I brushed my wet hood back and opened the swinging doors, stepping into the common room where a nurse was crossing the floor.

"May help you?" she asked, hugging a clipboard to her chest and cocking her head. "You don't look like one of our regulars."

"I'm not, I'm looking for Aileen O'Sullivan. Is it alright if I pop in and visit her a minute?"

"You must be here to say happy birthday," she said, smiling. "We've had a lot of visitors for her today. She's actually out at The Criterion Café right now, having a little birthday celebration. Everyone is welcome, so don't be afraid to go find her there."

The Criterion was eight blocks away, and I was pooped. But I had come so far, I couldn't fathom giving up. I thanked the nurse and left.

Just as I walked down the wheelchair ramp and onto the sidewalk, my phone rang. I picked it out of my bag and answered it without looking at the screen. "Hello?"

"Poppet?"

Liz was the last person that I wanted to be talking to at this point in time. I was tired, filthy, grumpy, scared, and just about at the end of my rope.

"Hello, Liz," I said. I got a chill from my own voice.

"You sound strange."

Irritation flared. "So do you," I said, abruptly. I wasn't actually paying attention to how she sounded, I was too distracted by my own problems. "Now is not really a good time, Liz."

Rain sprinkled into my face and I yanked my hood up again.

"You said that last time," she answered.

I couldn't exactly explain to my mother what was happening so I switched tactics. "I'm doing good. Is there something I can help you with?"

"Well..." She took a long pause.

I wasn't in the mood for long pauses. My feet were eating up the sidewalk between Sunny Valley Pensioners Home and The Criterion Café. I had a mission and speaking with Liz wasn't helping me accomplish it. I don't say that to excuse my behavior, just to gently remind you of my state of mind. So when Liz said, "I was wondering if you might like to come home early," I nearly went apoplectic.

I stopped dead on the sidewalk, rain dripping from the edge of my hood and into my face, running shoes soaked through. "Excuse me?"

She either didn't catch the fury in my tone, or she chose to ignore it. In either case, she barreled onward. "Yes. I was thinking that maybe it was a mistake to send you away for the entire summer. I've been so busy at work these past few months..."

"You mean years..." I seethed.

"Yes, years. Exactly. I've been thinking maybe it's time that you and I spend a little one on one time together, before the summer is out."

On another day, under a sunny sky, and maybe when I didn't have thoughts of broken hearts, a woman abandoned on the road, and my own doom hanging over my head, I would have reacted differently. But Liz had chosen the wrong moment, the wrong words, and the wrong daughter to do a 180 on. The conversation from that moment on went something like this:

"Coming to Ireland was your idea."

"I know, but..."

"You couldn't *wait* to get rid of me." My voice was getting louder.

"That's not true..."

"You foisted me off on your sister." My consonants were getting sharper. I may have spat on the word 'foisted.'

"I didn't foist—"

"Whose letters you never even bothered to read."

"I haven't had—"

"Who adopted a boy, a nephew you haven't bothered to meet or even ask about."

"Now hold on, that's not fair."

"You have no idea what's going on here right now, what you're interrupting." I yelled this.

"Well, if you'll just tell me then I'll—"

"You call up out of the blue, without any sensitivity or respect for what's happening in my life."

"Georjayna... Poppet."

It's only fair of me to report honestly that she never once raised her voice, or sounded defensive or angry. Too bad I was too furious to notice.

"And expect me to drop everything, turn around, get on a plane..."

"Well, yes but, no."

"Because you've had an attack of conscience about having neglected your daughter since she was eleven, and you think now would be a good time to try and make up for it." These words I definitely spat, like rusty nails.

The line was silent.

"Do I have it about right, *Liz*?" All of the venom that had built up over the last six years since she'd made partner, all of the anger and frustration, came out on her name. It was pregnant to bursting with an ugly hurt-baby.

There was an odd sort of wheeze on the other end of the phone, and some urgent talking in the background, the sounds of an office. I heard Liz's voice but I couldn't understand any of her words. It sounded like she had her hand over the mouthpiece. She hadn't even been listening to me.

I glared at my cell, ground my teeth, hung up the phone, and kept walking.

CHAPTER 28

I pushed open the cafe door and the sound of a crowd buzzed in my ears. I beelined for their washroom and washed my filthy hands, scrubbing hard with the soap and digging under my nails.

Once I was somewhat presentable, I went to the counter and ordered a cinnamon bun and a cup of tea. I ignored the snotty look of the young girl behind the counter. I must have still looked like a vagabond, but I didn't care.

"Heated?" she asked, lifting her chin but dropping her eyes, looking down her nose.

"No, thanks," I said.

She put the bun on a napkin and pushed it toward me with her tongs.

As I tore into the pastry like a starving person, a very loud off-key refrain of “Happy Birthday” startled me. Bingo. I craned my neck and spotted a crowd of gray-haired people, mostly women, at the very back of the cafe. A shiny red banner had been fixed in the corner - *Happy 100th Birthday!* A young woman holding a cake with a single sparkler on it lowered the concoction onto a table in the middle of a crowd of seniors.

Aileen was turning one hundred years old.

I chewed my way through my cinnamon bun and drank my tea. Both things tasted like ashes. I stole frequent glances toward the back of the cafe. Every few minutes, someone attending the party would leave. Sometimes they were a couple of old ladies, arms twined at the elbow, helping each other walk. Sometimes it was a single person, shuffling their way through the cafe and out the door. Felt hats, comfortable loafers, hose and skirts or wool slacks dominated the fashion choices. All of them looked old enough to be my grandparents, maybe even my great grandparents. The geriatric crowd was getting thinner and thinner.

When there was almost no partiers left I screwed up the courage and made my way to the back of the café .

When I saw her, I knew it was Aileen. She was by far the eldest of any of the people I'd seen here today. She sat in an advanced looking electric wheelchair. A much younger woman hovered nearby, the one who'd held the cake. Nurse? Daughter? Granddaughter? The last two partiers were pulling on cardigans with shaking hands, and finding their way to their feet.

"Excuse me," I said to the younger woman. She walked away from the table and approached me. I smiled warmly, even though every nerve was twanging. I gestured to Aileen. "Is that the lady turning a century old today?"

She smiled. "She is. Unbelievable, isn't it? I can't believe we let her out, but when a woman turns a hundred, you do whatever you can to grant her birthday wishes. She's still as spry as anyone, if you can believe it."

"Let her out?" I echoed, picturing a cell.

She laughed. "That sounds terrible, doesn't it? I just mean from the home. She wanted to come here to celebrate her birthday because she opened this cafe about sixty-five years ago. Course, it was a restaurant in those days."

"Really? That's amazing. I was wondering if I could sit and chat with her. Wish her happy birthday? Would you mind? It's not every day I meet someone who's lived one hundred years."

"Be my guest. She loves young people." She stepped aside and made room for me to sit down next to Aileen. "I'm just going to run to the loo, I'll be right back," she half-whispered.

As I sat, Aileen's head inclined in my direction. "Who's there?" she said in a dry, weak voice. Her eyes were filmy with white, her white hair a thin fluff around the crown of her head. Her nose was still straight and perfect, the only part of her face that looked untouched by the fingers of age.

"My name is Georjayna Sutherland," I said. "Happy birthday, Aileen."

A smile tugged at one corner of her withered lips. "Thank you. You sound funny. Where are you from?"

"I'm Canadian."

"Ah," she said, turning her head even more in my direction, her unseeing eyes unmoving in their sockets. One eyelid drooped. "I have family who moved to Canada after the war, but I never made it there myself." Her accent was strong, and I had to work to understand. "Even if you live for a century, it seems there is never time enough."

"I was wondering," I said, licking my lips, "if I might ask you something of a personal nature?"

"I'd welcome it," she said. "No one asks me anything about myself these days. One time, a journalist came to talk to me on my ninety-fifth birthday. But since then, I haven't had much excitement. Ask away."

I cleared my throat. "Are you married to a man named Cormac O'Brien?"

She didn't respond. Not even a blink. I couldn't read any expression in her blind eyes. She'd turned into a wax figure. My heart began to pound. "Ma'am? Aileen?"

"How do you know that name?" Her frail voice had gone so quiet, I had to lean in.

"I...well, I stumbled across it in the diary of a relative. And I stumbled across the name Aileen, too. I thought the reference might be to you."

"Which relative? Who are you related to?" Her voice wavered, but she didn't seem fearful.

"Mailís Stiobhard-Sheehan," I said, fumbling over the pronunciation, my eyes glued to her face.

"Oh," she said, and raised one shaking hand to her lips. "Stiobhard." She pronounced it Steward. "I have not heard that name in...I don't know how long. That poor, poor woman."

"Did you know her?"

Aileen's chaperone returned from the washroom. "I should be getting Aileen home, she tires easily," she said.

"Oh." I couldn't bring myself to stand. I was trying to think of how to ask for more time when Aileen spoke.

"Wait, Sarah," she said. "Just a few more minutes. I'm fine. Would you mind giving us a bit of privacy?"

Sarah looked surprised and shot me a wary look. "If you wish. I'll be over by the counter, then."

"Thanks," I said, relieved. I turned all of my attention to Aileen.

"I didn't know her very well," Aileen said. "But when I was a girl, everyone knew about Mailís. She went missing. I'm sure you know."

"Yes," I said. Did Aileen know why? Surely she couldn't be ignorant of what had thrown Mailís into an emotional hell-hole.

"She took her own life, poor soul."

"That's what they say." I didn't want to ask her outright. Was it fair of me to stir up the past for this elderly woman? But I didn't have to.

"She was meant to marry Cormac," came the frail voice.

"Your husband," I supplied.

"No. Cormac and I never married, although we intended to. Cormac died before we could. It's a long time ago, now. There was a time when I couldn't talk about any of this. But now it seems almost like it happened to someone else, it's so long ago. It was unacceptable at the time for a girl to get pregnant out of wedlock. Now, things are much different. But then, when I found out I was pregnant, and Eoin was killed in a political skirmish, I was completely lost. I couldn't tell my parents. I couldn't tell anyone, except Cormac."

"Eoin?" I said, sitting up with a start.

"Yes, my fiancé at the time. Cormac's brother."

Wait. What? "It wasn't Cormac's baby?"

She coughed out a laugh, "Goodness, no. I had no interest in Cormac that way. And he had none in me. We were friends. He was the only other person besides Eoin who knew about the baby. So when Eoin was killed..."

"Cormac stepped in to marry you..." I finished, my entire body was covered in gooseflesh. "Did Cormac love Mailís?" I asked, scanning the wrinkled face, the sightless eyes.

"Oh yes," she said. "Very much. He would have died for her. But in those days, duty to family was more important than love. After Eoin died, Cormac broke his engagement with her to marry me. He wanted his brother's child to have a father, and he wanted to protect me from the shame of it."

"What happened to him?"

"Do you see a black purse sitting nearby?" she asked, raising a hand.

I looked at the bench behind her. "Yes, here."

"Inside, you'll find a wallet. I don't mind if you open it."

I felt weird, rifling through the bag of an old blind lady. I pulled out a matching black wallet. "What am I looking for?"

"In the middle. Be careful, it's fragile."

In the very center of the wallet was a pocket. A soft yellowed paper had been folded up and slipped inside a plastic sleeve.

"I have carried this article around with me for over sixty years," she said. "In memory of Cormac. How such a good man could have gone in such a way, shakes me to my very soul. He should never have bought that property."

Property. Another piece of the puzzle slipped into place, and it was like an icy finger slipping down my spine. Cormac O'Brien. The O'Brien Property. Brendan - Jasher's father. He'd bought the O'Brien property, he was the current owner. He also seemed to have inherited some pretty terrifying bats. I kept my horror and shock inside as I gingerly unfolded the article.

Another newspaper clipping. My life had become a laundry line of frail newspaper articles. The black and white photograph at the top made my breath stop in my throat. A mummified body lay face down on the ground, one arm stretched out over its head. The wasted limb was no thicker than bone, the reaching hand and fingers nothing but a curled claw. A row of dead plants cradled one side of the body, like it had been unearthed from a neglected garden. The headline read: *Garda Baffled by Desiccated Body in Back Yard.*

"This is Cormac?" I whispered. I cleared my throat. "I don't understand how this is even possible in Ireland? I mean, he... " I stopped myself from saying that he looked like a mummy that had been unearthed from an Egyptian tomb.

"He's all dried out," said Aileen. "I lost my eyesight, but I can still see the image in my mind. It's impossible in a wet place such as Ireland. And even more impossible to have happened in one day. I'm telling you, it's that land." In a whisper, she added, "Cursed."

"One day?" I blinked. "What do you mean one day?" I looked down at the article and scanned for a date. "6 March, 1935."

"The day before that photo was taken, Cormac was seen by no less than a dozen people, alive and well. You see why it is the greatest mystery of Anacullough? Maybe even all of Ireland."

"This happened on his land? This is his garden?"

She nodded.

"The O'Brien place," I said. The image of bat-like creatures made of smoke flying out of Brendan's body rumbled noisily into my mind like a truck carrying a load of rocks. My hands trembled. Bad energy, Faith had said. I looked down at the mummified body, the dried lips laying the teeth bare. My heart thudded. This was a lot worse than bad energy.

"Do you mind if I take a photo of this article?" I asked Aileen.

"I don't mind," she said. "Many people have. Mostly journalists, over the years."

"Thank you." I took out my phone and laid the article out flat. I hovered over it, focusing, and captured it. I folded it up and put it back into her wallet.

"Thanks for talking with me, Aileen. I'll let you go home and rest now."

She nodded. "It was nice talking to you, Georjayna."

"Happy birthday, Aileen." I laid a hand on her skinny shoulder and she patted the back of my hand with a dry palm. I caught Sarah's eye and she left her chair by the counter and returned. Her face was loaded with curiosity.

"Thank you, I appreciate the time you gave me with her," I said.

Sarah opened her mouth, but I just gave her arm a squeeze and kept walking. My heart was pounding, and my throat felt dry and hot as the image of Cormac's skeletal hand, clutching at air, burned behind my eyes.

CHAPTER 29

When I left the cafe, the rain had stopped once again. The air had a fresh, humid quality and smelled extra green. I was so distracted by the strange conversation with Aileen that I don't remember the long walk back to the bike rack.

I took the handlebars, lifted the front tire from the rack, and pointed it toward home. A heavy exhaustion had settled in. I felt like I'd been running all over the county like a madwoman. Just as I was about to throw my leg over the bike, I noticed a woman with her back to me on the sidewalk, standing by a lamppost as though frozen.

Movement beyond her caught my eye and I looked past her. I gasped. Jasher's father stood in the square by the fountain, swaying on his feet. A swarm of the smoky bats flew around and through him. My hand flew to my mouth and my eyes stretched wide, I felt like they might pop out of my face. There were so many more demon bats than there had been before. He flailed an arm as though to knock a bat away, but his movement was aimless. It was obvious that he couldn't see them, only sense them. Brendan wore a gray trench coat in spite of the warmth of the day, and it hung on his shoulders the way it would a scarecrow. He was wasting away.

"O'Brien," I whispered. Brendan had lost at least thirty pounds since I'd seen him outside the library, maybe more. How did a man lose that much weight in a matter of days? A chill crept across the backs of my hands.

A metallic crash made me jump and snapped me out of my theorizing. The woman turned to look at me. "Alright there, miss?" she said, her Irish lilt warm and friendly.

I picked the bike up and jammed it back into the bike rack just to give myself a second to catch my breath. My eyes were drawn back to Brendan like he was magnetized. "Yes, sorry."

The woman turned her back to me. I walked to stand beside her and realized she was staring at Brendan, too. Could she see the smoky black shapes? Highly unlikely, but they were so clear to me that it was hard to believe no one else could see them.

"Do you know him?" I asked.

"Aye, I did," she said, not taking her eyes from Brendan.

A beat.

"What do you see?" I asked, hesitantly.

She didn't seem surprised by the question. "I see a very sad story," she answered. "Very sad. He was once a pillar in our community. Now look at him."

I was looking. Brendan flailed an arm at a darting black shape that flew a circle around his head and then disappeared into his neck in a puff of black powder, like a fungus exploding and sending spores everywhere. I shuddered. A few guttural and angry words came across the square from him, words that make no sense to me. Gaelic?

"You see what heartbreak can do to you if you let it? He could have kept that precious boy. He could have accepted that bad things sometimes happen and it's no one's fault. He could have survived. Thrived even."

I tore my eyes from Brendan to look at her pale face, her blue eyes sad. "This all started after he bought Cormac O'Brien's place?"

She nodded and glanced at me. "You're a foreigner, how do you know?"

"Jasher is my adopted cousin," I said.

Her face lit. "Ah, so you're Faith's niece. Come from Canada are you?"

"Yes, just for the summer." My eyes went back to Brendan. "What's wrong with him?"

She gazed at him, not seeing what I was seeing, but it didn't matter. It was obvious something was very wrong with him. She shook her head. "No one can help him now. You watch. He'll end up just like that O'Brien man. Swallowed up in the dead earth of that place. It's a grim business, that." She gave a sad nod and shuffled away.

I was nailed to the cobblestone by her words. *Swallowed up in the dead earth of that place.* The dried out corpse of Cormac wavered before my eyes, a transparent image overlaying the man now staggering across the square, the smoky bats swooping after, around, and through him. I left the bike and followed him, staying well back. He walked like a drunken man, muttering to himself, occasionally swinging an arm out at a pest he couldn't see.

People who saw Brendan coming crossed the street to get away from him. He had deteriorated fast. I could hardly reconcile this lost soul with the man I'd seen at the beginning of the summer outside the grocery store.

Brendan turned a corner I jogged so I wouldn't lose sight of him. As I followed, my mind was a crashing sea of questions. What did the woman mean by *dead earth*? Could the earth have taken vengeance on Cormac because of Mailís? She was a Wise, a being gifted by the ancient fae. Had the fae taken deadly steps to avenge her broken heart? Somehow, I couldn't see the fae being so malicious, they were life-givers, not life-takers.

Brendan walked slowly and I stayed back as I followed him through a residential area. The houses soon thinned, each successive yard larger than the last. The energy of the earth hummed beneath the soles of my shoes, vibrating and alive. We were leaving Anacullough.

Brendan meandered down a long, tree-lined road. Most of the small, gnarly trees in the ditch were covered in crab apples. I stayed back and kept to the moist shoulder to muffle my footsteps. I wondered if he knew where he was going or if he'd decided he just wanted a walk. He seemed to amble aimlessly at points, and every so often an arm would flash out at a bat. The road wound through pastureland. There were very few farmhouses now, mostly fences, stone cairns, and sheep.

I knew we'd arrived not because Brendan opened a wooden gate on squeaky hinges and entered a yard, but because of how that yard looked. The house must have been beautiful once; it had been a stone bungalow with wooden trim. Now, it was crumbling, with one corner of the foundation half sunk into the ground.

I now understood what the woman had meant by *dead earth*. Nothing grew on the property. Nothing. Not a weed, not a tree, not a mushroom. Nothing. The earth around the house looked as gray as ash and dry as desert sand. Vibrant green surrounded the plot of land on all sides, the dead land stretched out in a circle with an abrupt edge - thick green grass outside the circle, poisoned looking earth inside.

I could sense at the very edges of my being that there was no life in the earth under this house, or around it. I watched Brendan stagger up a path he'd packed down by his daily comings and goings. With each step, a cloud of black dust drifted up around his boot, like fine powder. The black dust clung to his clothing like mold. He took a wild swing at a demon-bat in the air and spun in a circle with a loud cry. My hand flew to my throat and tears pricked my eyes. The hand that flashed through the air was bony and gnarled. The demon-bat disappeared into his gut and he reacted like he'd been socked hard by an imaginary fist. Doubled over, Brendan staggered up the half-collapsed steps and fell through the door, slamming it behind him.

I squeezed my eyes shut and a hot tear escaped. I thought of Jasher and my heart ached for him. Who could help his father now?

CHAPTER 30

I looked down at the ashy dirt not far from my feet. From far away, the edge of the dry place formed an oblong shape, like how the circle of a flashlight bulb stretches into a long oval when the light hits at an angle. The patch of dead earth surrounded the house, swallowed up one side of the yard, and reached under the fence and out toward the dirt road. I stepped up to the edge, my flip flops only a few inches away from the depleted soil.

I squatted down to inspect the ground more closely. I sniffed. A faint smell of mold and putrefaction wrinkled my nose. I reached out, hesitated, then dipped a finger into what used to be earth but now seemed beyond definition. The gray substance clung to my finger. I rubbed my thumb against it and it smeared like ash, staining my skin. A wisp of smoke drifted up from my fingertips.

I eyeballed the house Brendan had gone into, took a deep breath, and drove my fingers down into the ash, scooping up a handful. I rose, trailing dust and smoke through my fingers. A residual appeared and my eyes found it easily, two transparent grainy figures moving in the yard. Residual garden plants and trees filled the yard and I could see the beauty the place had once had. Trees with thick trunks lined the edge of the property.

I gasped and took a step back. It was like sitting down in a movie theatre after the show had already begun, the action already far along. A residual of Mailís was approaching a residual of Cormac, her face twisted with rage, a hand, no, a claw reaching out toward the man. She wore the same high-necked black dress as she had been wearing on the road. Cormac, who had a hoe in his hand, dropped the tool as he turned and his entire body arched backward at an impossible angle. It was a silent horror show.

Cormac fell and Mailís strode forward, hand still reaching. Cormac's residual partially disappeared among the potato plants but I could see his limbs thrash as he died, and then became still.

A shockwave of realization went through me. Mailís was the murderous one. My ancestor had killed her lover. My chin trembled at the terrible sight and my blood turned to ice, but I could not look away. Mailís was not satisfied with only his death. Though I couldn't hear her, I knew she was screaming when her mouth dropped open and her body heaved with effort.

Cormac's hand and arm were just visible among the leaves and I gasped as I watched his hand wither and the plants around him shrink and die, exposing the rest of his corpse. Mailís did not stop. She stood over his body, desiccating it of fluid completely until it was truly nothing more than bone with a covering of skin. Even the hair dried out and bits of it blew on the breeze. The circle of desiccation spread out from Mailís but mostly forward and back of her. I watched, horrified, as trees shrank and toppled. Shrubs dried up like they were on fire, turning to dust. The decomposition process happened before my eyes like a time-lapse video.

Mailís stopped screaming, but her chest heaved as she looked down at the mummified body of Cormac and she didn't move for a long time. Tracks of tears glistened on her face, but her twisted countenance was barely recognizable as human. Her gaze finally moved away from the corpse to take in the damage around her. Her eyes widened in fear. I could see the understanding dawn on her face as she looked around at the destruction she had wrought. She looked at her hands, and around again. She put her hands on the top of her head and the terror on her face made fear blossom in my own heart, even though this event had happened more than a half-century ago and couldn't touch me.

Mailís turned, lifted her skirts, and ran toward the woods at the back of the house. I could see leaves and limbs through her form as she sprinted. My whole body jumped in surprise when Mailís hit an invisible barrier at the edge of the dry place and flew backward.

Before I could register fully what I had seen, the whole residual blinked out and started over at the beginning. Ghostly plants and trees once more filled the property. Cormac's form bent to his work, hoeing between his potato plants. Mailís appeared between the trees behind him, her face a mask of deathly intent. She only watched him from a distance, still, just a pair of angry eyes following his every movement.

I was surprised when a third figure appeared in the residual on my left. A pretty girl in a dress. "Aileen," I whispered. The girl's strong straight nose was the only thing that looked the same as it still did today. She was a beautiful girl, with long curly hair tied back in a ribbon. There was no color in the residual but I could tell that it was a bright golden yellow, like wheat.

Mailís's face became a thunderous storm cloud as Aileen approached Cormac. He took a break from his weeding to stand and talk with Aileen for a few moments. Aileen began to weep, putting her hands up to her face, and then moved one to her belly where her pregnancy would soon show. Cormac pulled a kerchief from his shirt pocket and gave it to her. He wrapped an arm around her shoulders and kissed her temple, like a big brother might. He comforted her with words I couldn't hear and Aileen nodded, wiped her face with his kerchief, and kissed his cheek. The whole energy between them made Aileen's words in The Criterion ring true.

Residual Aileen left Cormac to his gardening. Cormac and Mailís both watched her go, one with concern on his face and the other with ugly jealousy. Cormac bent his forehead to rest on the backs of his hands on the top of the hoe and I thought he might be praying. The poor man had just lost his brother. I wondered how long before this scene had the one on the road taken place. Maybe it had even been the same day?

Mailís's eyes tracked Aileen's departure long after she'd stepped out of the residual scene. Hands balled at her sides, Mailís marched out of the trees. She crossed the property and said something to Cormac, who turned in surprise. Her claw-like hand was already lifting as he turned, and the scene continued where I'd entered it first.

I watched the entire thing unfold one more time, dread freezing my blood as I thought about what this could mean. Mailís was going through the process of becoming a Wise, just like me. A Wise was gifted with the power to heal and nourish life, so how had she managed to use her ability for something so shockingly the opposite?

When Mailís bounced off the invisible wall and the residual reset itself, I lowered my hand and dropped the ashy dirt back to the ground. She hadn't gone missing, she'd become trapped here. The residual faded away as I dusted off my hands, but I couldn't entirely rid my skin of the awful stain it left behind.

Calmly, I took out my phone and dialed the house.

"Hello?" Jasher answered.

"It's Georjie," I said, my eyes on the dark house, worry for the man inside writhing in my guts. "Can you meet me at the O'Brien place? Now. It's important."

CHAPTER 31

While I waited for Jasher, I wandered into the ditch and plucked a crab apple from one of the cluster of trees along the side of the road.

I looked down at the shiny red fruit, and all of its mineral and vitamin content became information that fed into my skin. I could heal scurvy with this fruit, and bladder infections, and athlete's foot, and a host of other diseases. I held the apple, balancing it on the ends of my fingertips. I pulled the nourishment into me, feeling the love between the properties of the fruit and my body. I gazed at the fruit with affection and it seemed to gleam in response. It was full of super-powered water and bursting with nourishment. I could draw resources from the apple without hurting the fruit itself, but I was taking from it with love and appreciation. What if I took from a place of malice instead? What would happen to the apple then?

I purposefully turned my thoughts to Liz. I thought of how she'd distanced herself from me after she'd made partner, the new and prestigious role in her life gradually taking my place in her affections and attentions. I thought of how she hadn't even tried to hide that she wanted me gone for the summer, how it would be easier for her if I wasn't there, then how she'd changed her mind when it was convenient for her. I thought of how she had her secretary take care of my personal stuff - booking my doctor's appointments, chauffeuring me around before I'd gotten my license, sending me reminders about tests and deadlines coming up. I released all of the anger, betrayal, and feelings of abandonment that I usually kept tightly sealed up in a watertight compartment.

I sucked the nourishment out of the apple again and this time, it began to shrivel. The skin wrinkled and dried up as its life drained into my fingers. It was so easy. So unbelievably easy. A cocktail of negative emotions filled my heart and my healing powers turned deadly. I narrowed my eyes at the Liz-apple, and kept pulling. Deep folds appeared as I drained the moisture. The apple puckered in on itself, turned brown. I didn't stop until it was nothing but a dried out, brittle core. A tear slipped down my cheek and I brushed it away. My chest heaved and my heart pounded. Another tear fell.

What became of a Wise when she used her abilities for taking instead of giving? For killing instead of reviving? Nausea twisted my stomach and made my mouth water. A small, niggling sensation pushed its way through the nausea. It felt as if something was vacuuming my breath from my body and sucking at my face and forehead. Terrified, I stopped draining the apple. My breath came in pants, but the sick suction-like feeling passed.

I was angry with Liz. But I didn't hate her, I loved her. In spite of the chasm between us, she was still my mother. I could easily desiccate an apple with the negative emotion I felt when I thought of her. So what could I do if I really hated someone? Mailís had demonstrated the terrifying answer to that question. Something Akiko had said to me once rang in my memory. *You can't really hate someone unless you've loved them first.* You might feel revulsion, or anger, or indifference, or any number of negative feelings toward a rude stranger, but hate was reserved for a special circumstance. It was reserved only for those whom we have loved, but who have betrayed our love at the deepest level.

"What are you doing?" Jasher's voice was full of alarm, and I started.

I hadn't even noticed when he pulled the truck over to the side of the road and parked it on the shoulder. He'd left the door open and come to stand near me. I had been standing there holding a desiccated apple and probably looking a bit stunned.

A warm hand touched my upper back. "Georjie, talk to me."

I turned to Jasher. Two more hot tears left tracks on my cheeks. His eyes were full of me. I squeezed my eyes shut and brushed away the tears. The dried out corpse in the garden flashed behind my eyelids. If Mailís was capable of that, then I was, too. We weren't any different. Suddenly I wanted nothing more than to pass the powers I'd been given back to the fae, to beg them to take back their breath, to choose someone else.

But what came out of my mouth was, "We have to get your father out of there."

Jasher's face hardened, not at me but at my words. He turned toward the black dust, the crumbling house. I grabbed him inside the crook of his elbow, trying to hold him back.

"No, Jasher. Don't cross that line. Whatever has taken up residence in the space and is possessing your father, will possess you, too."

His eyes widened. With a big breath, he cried out, "Da."

Both of us ran until our toes were on the edge of the grass, and yelled for Brendan.

I nearly sank to my knees with relief when the front door to the house opened and Brendan came out onto the porch. He swayed unsteadily on his feet, and an arm flew through the air as a demon that circled him once disappeared into his shoulder.

"Did you see that?" I asked.

Jasher shook his head, but he hissed through his teeth. "No, but I don't have to see anything to understand that he's dying. I don't know what seeing me is going to do to him, though. He couldn't handle it even on his best days. That's why I haven't seen him in years. I knew he bought this place, but I never saw..." Then it was like something sunk into his brain. Jasher put cold hands on my shoulders and made me face him. His eyes were wild. "What do you mean 'whatever has taken up residence'? What has taken up residence here?"

"Mailís," I choked out.

As though in response to her name, black dust drifted up from the ground. I grabbed Jasher by the arm, squeezing tight.

"Da! Come to us, now," Jasher yelled.

Brendan shook his head like a dog who had heard something too high-pitched for his sensitive hearing. He staggered sideways and took a drunken step off the porch and onto the stairs, nearly falling down them.

Jasher's eyes were on his father, while I couldn't tear mine away from the gathering smoke and swirling cloud of dust. Brendan took a few more steps, tripped on the bottom step, and stumbled to his knees. Jasher surged forward again, and I fought to hold him back.

"Let me go, Georjie. He won't make it on his own."

The black dust condensed, and lost its transparency. It drew into itself and formed a shape, a pillar. Jasher saw it, too, and we both shrank back as a wraith rose from the dry place. Behind it, several bats emerged from Brendan, along with a keening noise I hoped I'd never hear again. It made every hair on my body stand at attention.

Jasher looked at me, his eyes wild in his face. "You know their names, Georjie. Call them."

I knew immediately who he meant. The fae. Before I could stop him, Jasher took off across the dead yard towards his father. I stumbled as he yanked his arm from my grasp. Jasher sprinted across the yard, cutting around the darkening shape. As he passed the wraith, spectral black tentacles formed and licked out toward him. Jasher's back arched and he cried out as though whipped. He reached his father's side and slid in the dust like a baseball player going for home plate. Brendan was gibbering nonsense and began to swing at his son as wildly as he had swung at the bats. Jasher ducked his strikes while trying to haul his father to his feet. I could hear him speaking to his father in Gaelic. His voice was a strange hybrid of soothing and urgent.

The wraith grew bigger, with flashing black arms like ropes whipping out from its center. It had no real face, just a dense spindle shape with flailing tentacles like an octopus. The feeling snapping in the air was a hopeless despair and a desperate loneliness and regret. Not in my hearing but in my brain, I heard a terrifying screech. At a loss for what else to do, I began to call the names of the fae.

CHAPTER 32

Jasher and Brendan now both appeared drunk. An urgency overtook me – I needed to get them out of there. Immediately. The bats were having a heyday, dive bombing Jasher as well as his father, the smoky bodies disappearing and reappearing.

Despite the urgency inside that I help them, I stood my ground on the grass. I couldn't help them if I was overcome as well. The only thing I could think to do was call the fae. I called name after name from memory, beginning with the names from my dream. The oldest fae. In theory, the most powerful fae. Surely if anyone had the strength to beat back this wraith, it was those spirits of nature - they were the wraith's very opposite.

Colored lights began to flash in my periphery, through the trees in the woods beyond the property. Relief made my limbs feel weak. They were coming.

The tentacles of the wraith had found Jasher and Brendan. Brendan was on his knees. Jasher was on his feet, but his body was bowed at an awkward angle, and an arm flashed out at the air, trying in vain to ward off the tentacles of the black specter.

I continued to call names, one after the other. The lights in the distance grew closer, and more joined from the ground, from the leaves. Even from the stones they rose. When the first of the faerie lights crossed the property border, I forgot myself and stopped calling to watch, expecting the wraith to shrink back into the earth.

But what was I seeing? The lights crossed the property line, sped up, hit the wraith, and disappeared in little clouds of colored vapor. My brain couldn't make sense of what my eyes were seeing. Were they going to attack her from the inside? My eyes fell on Brendan and Jasher. They were both on the ground now. Jasher's hair had begun to turn gray.

"No," I whispered. My veins felt as if they were filled with ice chips. It wasn't working. The fae looked like they were getting sucked in and destroyed. It was a void, an empty dry place where the fae could not live. How could it be that they were not stronger than it?

Before my very eyes, Jasher was losing weight. Brendan was already skeletal.

"No!" I screamed this time. I called more fae, frantically. Name after name I called, hoping that it would be sheer numbers that would defeat the black demon. More lights appeared from the woods, crossing the hills and valleys and twinkling, seemingly happy to come to my service.

But it was in vain. They disappeared, one after another, into the black void, and without a sound. I stopped calling and took a big breath. I couldn't believe what I was seeing. "Stop! Stop, stop!" I yelled, "it's a vacuum!" and the lights stopped flying towards the void. Anger and desperation filled me. I closed my eyes. I was going to have to fight, but how? These powers didn't come with an owner's manual.

One thing I did know was that I couldn't come from hate. That was how Mailís had turned out this way. I might end up just like her – a murderous wraith – if I let my fear and anger overcome me. I opened my eyes, and a cry tore from my lips. Jasher lay in the dirt. His once beautiful muscular forearm was propped up at his side. I could see the fine carpal bones through the back of his hand, and the hollow between the bones of his forearm. All of my ability to draw healing energies felt useless and I was running out of time. I had to get them out of there. I bolted toward Jasher, but as I reached the border between the grass and the ash, and leapt into the space above the dry place, the wraith hit me.

There was no warning. Nothing I had ever experienced in my life up until then could ever have prepared me for a hit like that. The breath was stolen from the hollow of my mouth and not so much squeezed from my lungs by compression as sucked out by vacuum. I left half my IQ hanging in the air where my head used to be as I flew right out of my shoes. I soared like I'd been lobbed from a catapult and hit Jasher's truck broadside. My head whipped back and every muscle running from my right collarbone to my right ear stretched and then snapped. I heard a sound like a breaking carrot. I dropped to the ground just behind the front tire, a heap of unattached bones.

A high-pitched whine rang in both ears, and behind that, the violent shriek of the wraith, far away and fuzzy, like it had cotton stuffed into its windpipe. The tacky flesh of my lungs stuck together, and no matter how hard I sucked I could not draw breath. My body twitched with the effort.

I lay there for years. Faith and Liz grew old and passed on. Jasher and Brendan joined Cormac among the ranks of the mummified dead. Targa and Saxony stood at each other's weddings, a space at their elbow that should have been mine. Long shadows of tree limbs overhead passed over my body a thousand times. Targa gave birth to a set of twins, while Saxony traveled the world. Akiko...

As I lay there feeling death's shadow cool my skin, my crippled organs pulsing weakly, I realized that I had no predictions for Akiko's future. Had I ever really known my friend? Hadn't I failed her, somehow, by not knowing her? And what about Liz? I had been so unforgiving, so rigid. I, who had prided myself on my compassion, had been so without compassion for my own mother. Jasher's face swam in my vision behind the clouds drifting across the sky. His eyes when he looked at Brendan were filled only with love, even after all the abuse he'd endured. If he could find it within himself to have compassion for his father, couldn't I do the same for my mother? Shame burned within me.

Tears leaked from the outside corners of my eyes and tracked into my hairline. The tickles crawling over the fine hairs and pores drew me back to the present. My lungs finally relaxed enough for the vacuum to release and I sucked in a ragged breath and choked. My spine. My right kidney. Nothing was normal beneath the surface of my skin.

Move. Georjayna. Get up. They're dying.

I coughed and panted. The pain was excruciating. But oxygen cleared my thinking like a heavy wind pushes clouds away from the moon. My head lolled and I saw the underside of the truck and the grasses on the other side. Plant life. If I could draw their energy to me... I threw an arm toward the green-filled ditch. My body rolled and my legs flopped out. I drew my legs up, bent my knees, and lay my naked soles flat against the earth.

Thick, ropy roots shot from my soles and down deep into the ground, ploughing through the soil, penetrating the topsoil and driving into the pedolith. The world exploded. Colored light lit every plant, every tree around me. My pain dissolved and broken-ness mended as knowledge poured through the soles of my feet, filled my entire being, and opened areas in my brain I never even knew were lying dormant.

A new sensation filled me, so powerful that I was sure that my hair was standing on end. My body unfolded toward the sky like a sapling, drawing nourishment from the organic matter beneath me. I grew and didn't stop. The truck and the dead land and the house shrank below as I became like a thick oak, huge and strong, with roots penetrating layers of subsoil and clay and humus, every strata offering unique rich and nourishing properties. I kept growing in both directions. My roots felt as though they had no end and the sun filtered life in through my skin.

Looking down, the wraith was a black smudge of smoke, and the ashen earth around it a sandy hole of putrefaction. Two men foundered in the gray ash, feeble creatures in peril below the giant sequoia that I had become. Odd, I thought. Neither the wraith who had been Mailís, nor the father or the son looked up at this massive redwood looking down at them.

Energy and nutrient-rich water pulsed through my roots and up through my limbs, into my organs and brain. Everything around me for miles was alive with life-force light. Every plant, tree, and shrub. The world had become a rainbow of shifting, pulsing light.

Beneath my roots and running straight to the left and the right of me was a bright white line of light. I had a sensation like swinging a big heavy head full of branches to look first left, then right. The white light shot straight as an arrow off to either horizon and was so bright that the light of it blotted out anything living in its path or erected on top of it. I squinted at its cool blue and yet bright-white light.

Way back in my consciousness, I heard a voice, so faint, like a bell sounding far away. It was Faith's voice.

...matrix of energy lines criss-crossing the earth...

My roots were deeply embedded in the white line of light. I pulled my attention back to the scene below me, feeling an urgency in the small people down there, people that I knew.

The hole of rot below had become nothing more to me than a tiny blight on the skin of an apple. The sort of dent you wouldn't even bother to cut out with a knife.

"Jasher," I said. A sound like thunder rumbled and rolled across the land. Was that me? I was too big, too powerful. Just the desire to be closer made my vision sharper and I narrowed in on the two dying men. Eight leafy vines shot from the soil and stretched toward Jasher and Brendan. Three of them penetrated the wraith and a distant scream filtered into my hearing. The green vines wrapped around the men, cradling them and lifting them from the mold-riddled sand. My vines. Like umbilical cords, they pulsed with the juices of the earth, feeding the men with healing nutrients from plants I sensed and selected from miles around. The men's bodies fattened and fleshed out, their skin grew plump and rosy. I couldn't register expressions on their faces, they were blurred and seemed to communicate in a language I might have understood once. My vines settled them into the grass and the two men landed on spring-loaded, energy-filled legs.

I turned my attention to the wraith and the rest of the world blurred away. What had seemed so huge and terrible now seemed small, petty, infirm, and frail.

CHAPTER 33

I stretched out my right hand, fingers spread. My huge sequoia limb swept forward, branches opening toward the wraith. My left arm - another massive branch, reached out to the other side. Time had slowed down and my movements had taken on the heavy, power-filled motions of a giant.

A cracking noise snapped across the landscape and echoed off the hills in the distance, and a slow groan vibrated like some giant rusty nail was being pried from a wooden board. I could feel the ground quaking through my roots. Two huge cracks formed in the earth as I raised two cliffs up out of the neighboring land on either side of the property. The dark house full of sucking death collapsed and slid toward the crevice. Black bats trailing smoke exploded from the windows and the cracks in the walls, swirling and flapping like they were drunk and panicked.

The wraith screamed, its dry place sifting and dissolving beneath the specter. The wraith shrank into itself, and the horror of its missing face melted into human-like features. Limbs formed from the dust and the shape of a woman was wrung from the shadow. I could almost make out the dress she'd been wearing when she'd trapped herself in this land for good.

"Mailís," I said, and her face cleared as she recognized her name. My voice rolled like an echo after a crack of thunder. Black bruises ringed her face and eyes, and what had once been a beautiful set of teeth were black pegs of rot. Her black eyes lightened, almost but not quite reaching a human shade of brown. "He loved you. Cormac loved who you used to be."

My mountains of earth towered on either side of her, hanging at impossible angles in the air and making her look so small. At my words the wraith paused, understanding the meaning. Regret poured off the being in waves, like heat wavering over desert sand. She threw her head back and cried an agonized scream to the sky. She turned black-ringed grief-filled eyes upward and opened ghostly arms and hands out to yield to her fate. As the two walls of earth and soil crashed over the house, there was an exhale of surrender soon drowned out by the heaving and groaning of the land. The earth churned and swallowed the wraith, the bats, the house, and the gritty, putrid ash. I rolled and tossed and mixed the soil, keeping my eyes locked there with intention.

"Georjie." A voice said a name from far away and off to the side. I heard it, and registered the name as mine.

The towering sequoia withdrew into me, my heavy limbs becoming light and fleshy once again. Only then did I become conscious that the roots shooting from the soles of my feet and reaching into the earth were not actual physical appendages, as I unconsciously lifted a foot from the earth.

The energy feeding into me from the strata below instantly halved in intensity and I wobbled, off balance. I set my foot down and stabilized myself. I stood there breathing, for I don't know how long. A hand unconsciously went to my head as I processed everything that had just happened. I looked down at myself... my limbs, my hands. I spread my fingers before me, open, long and beautiful. This was still my body. I was not a tree.

I looked down at my bare feet, dirty to the knees with soil. I smiled, and a hysterical laugh burbled up. I wriggled my toes and looked around myself for my flip flops. Nowhere to be found.

"Georjie."

I turned and looked up, my eyes falling on Jasher for the first time since I returned to myself. Was it just my imagination or had he gotten bigger?

"You look...healthy," I said. My voice cracked. "Have you seen my shoes?"

He mutely held out my flip flops and I walked over and took them. I dropped them onto the earth and slipped my dirty feet into them.

"I need a wash," I said, looking down at myself. But what would have driven me insane before, was now pleasurable.

I noticed my phone in his other hand, his tanned fingers curling around the pink case.

"Oh, thank you." I reached for it, and he lifted his hand and let me take it. Movement in my periphery drew my attention to the man standing just behind the truck box. "Hello," I said. "We've met before. You remember?"

"I do," he said in a rich, resonant bass voice. He looked younger, more vital than the man I had met on the street at the beginning of the summer. His eyes were no longer shuttered and clouded, but a clear and vibrant brown. He seemed frozen to the spot for a moment, but then shook himself and moved around the truck, reaching out a hand. "I'm sorry, I..." We grasped hands and shook, awkwardly, like we were at a house party instead of two people who had just survived a traumatic supernatural experience. "Nice to see you again," he said.

As the minutes passed, the revelation of what I had become and how much power had been at my disposal began to register. My body trembled. A fear-filled awe overcame me and spots flashed in front of my eyes. I reached out a blind hand. "Jasher?" My voice quavered and vertigo made the world spin.

"I'm here." A solid arm went around me just as my legs buckled, and he took the bulk of my weight. "I'm here, Georjie. I've got you."

"I can't see," I whispered, my fingers clutching at his shirt. His collarbones winged out under my hands and warm shoulder muscles jumped under my palms.

"Take a breath," he said, so close to my ear that I could feel the breath from his own lips.

I inhaled deeply through my nose, once, twice, and three times. The black cleared away from my vision and Jasher's face came into focus.

"You're alright," Jasher said, brushing my hair away from my face. His arm tightened around me as my legs found strength again and I stood. His brown eyes were soft, filled with compassion. But from the concern drawing his eyebrows together, I could tell that he didn't really believe I was alright.

"Take me home," I said.

CHAPTER 34

I'm not quite sure how, but I know it was all thanks to Jasher that I ended up properly in bed and properly asleep, until the silent faraway sound of a creak woke me. I was so dazed when I went to bed that night that I wasn't sure what was real and what wasn't.

When I woke, the room was still mostly dark. My mind was clear and my thoughts were no longer jumbled. My thoughts turned to Mailís, and I began to piece together the path that had led her to where she'd ended up. She'd never learned the full truth about why Cormac had left her, why he had broken her heart so brutally. She'd been convinced it was for another woman. I remembered the moment the horseman came flying into the residual to whisk Cormac away. I couldn't hear the words that were said, but it was clear that Cormac and Mailís had been interrupted. Had he intended to tell her the full reason and hadn't had the chance? I recalled the moment her body had bounced off some invisible barrier, after she'd killed Cormac. Had the fae locked her there? Had they seen how destructive she'd been with the powers they had given her and, unable to take them away, they simply put her in jail? Or had she done it to herself by sucking all the life out of the earth and making a void she couldn't leave? She'd still been there, still alive in a way. Did that mean I was immortal now too? How many others were there like me, and could I find someone with the answers to all of my questions?

There was another creak and I lifted my head to listen.

"Georjie?" It was Jasher, whispering at my door.

"Hey," I whispered back.

He padded into my room silently and approached my bed.

"Did I wake you?"

"No. Are you okay?" I went to sit up.

"Yes, yeah. It's alright. Stay down." The bed depressed as he crawled over to the space beside me and lay on his side facing me. I relaxed against my pillow, pushing the fabric under my cheek so I could see him.

He took my hand and squeezed it. His fingers were freezing.

"Why are you so cold?" I put my palm against his cheek, it was also frigid to the touch.

"I was outside." He caught my hand against his cheek and pressed it there.

"How come?"

"I had a lot of thinking to do," he said.

"Yeah." I could relate.

We lay facing each other in silence, but he was not restful. I could feel the energy pulsing through him. He kept squeezing and caressing my fingers, but in an agitated fashion.

"Can I tell you something?" he finally said, like he couldn't hold it in anymore.

"I wish you would," I answered.

"I can't see ghosts anymore."

A few heartbeats passed.

"What?" This time I did sit up.

He gave up the pretense of relaxing and sat up, too. "I'm not joking."

"How do you know? What if there aren't any ghosts around? I mean, what makes you think that you can't see them anymore?"

"There are always ghosts around, Georjie." He started talking with his hands. "I was downtown. At first I didn't notice, I was too...freaked out by what had happened. As we drove through Ana, my focus was just getting you home. But after you went to sleep, I got to thinking. There is this one ghost that always hangs out on the corner of Fleet, in front of O'Shea's Pub. He's never *not* there. For my whole life I've been avoiding that corner because of that ghost. I avoid all kinds of places in town because of the dead that haunt them. But, as we were driving home, I didn't see him there." His accent was getting thicker and he was talking faster. "It really began to weigh on me, so I took my bike out and went to Ana tonight, to check that corner, and all the other usual places, including Eithne."

"No ghosts?"

He shook his head, almost violently. "Not one."

Even in his whisper I could hear the excitement in his voice, feel it vibrating through him.

"It's not some kind of fluke?" I said, hope rustling in my chest like a bird about to take flight.

He took my hand again. "I think that whatever you did to me, when you saved me and my da's lives, you healed whatever had scarred me since my birth. I feel like a totally different person."

I was thunderstruck. I hoped it wasn't some sort of strange coincidence. That all the ghosts hadn't just decided to take a holiday last night. "That's incredible, Jasher."

"It's more than incredible, Georjie. It's life-changing. Do you know what this means?"

He was no longer bothering to whisper. Yes, I knew what it meant. It meant everything. To him, it literally meant the world. I could hear it in his voice.

"It means you can go to University, visit Rome, and Angkor Wat."

He nodded. He held my hand and stroked my cheekbone with his other. "It means I can live, Georjie. It means you've given me back my life."

"It wasn't me, Jasher. It was the fae that did it."

He shook his head. "Maybe they gave you the power you have, made you what you are."

I'm a Wise, now. Whatever that means.

"But this gift came through you." His palm caressed my cheek. "Thank you."

I didn't know what to say. I couldn't take credit for whatever I had been able to do. I hadn't even been conscious that it was happening, I just didn't want Jasher to be desiccated to death the way Cormac had been. I wished I could go back in time and save Cormac, too.

"I need to kiss you," he said, suddenly. "Can I kiss you?"

Part of me had always thought men were being wimps when they asked that, but I detected a hidden meaning in his question. "You already have kissed me, Jasher. Twice. Have you forgotten?"

"No I haven't," he said. "Not at all." And with that, he closed the space between us and took my lips with his. A strong arm wrapped around my lower back and pulled me to him, right onto his lap.

He splayed his hand on my upper chest, over my heart, the fingertips pressing into my skin like he wanted to feel what it was made of. His hand slid up my chest, over my collarbones, along my neck and curved around the base of my skull. He wound his fingers through my hair and turned my head, deepening the kiss. His stubble scraped against my face.

Now I knew what a lit match felt like. The kiss ignited and consumed us. I wrapped my arms around his neck and upper back, the muscles jumping under my hands. It was the pure vulnerability and generosity in the kiss that melted my bones into a warm liquid. Never had I been kissed in such a soul-baring, defenseless manner. As his mouth moved against mine, I was beginning to wonder if I had ever been kissed at all. Some kisses take, some kisses give. This kiss entrusted and endowed. I felt like a rich woman.

I knew Jasher couldn't be mine, at least not then. He had been given an escape. All of the closed doors surrounding him had just swung wide, and the fresh, clean air of opportunity had wafted in. This man, this talented, compassionate soul, would make an impact on the world.

Jasher and I had been through a lot. But even through all the wonderful moments we'd shared, there had always been a wall around him. His self-preservation box. During this kiss, and only then, did he give himself all to me. That's what I mean about generosity. He laid bare his soul and I basked in its beauty. Everyone deserves to be kissed the way Jasher kissed me that night. If you haven't been yet, you will, and then you'll know what I mean.

We broke the kiss and became still, our faces so close together my skin tingled. Our breathing was the only sound for a long time.

"You're extraordinary," he said, and the words skipped off his tongue. Funny, I'd been thinking the same thing about him. But I no longer had the presence of mind to bring two words together, let alone a multisyllabic word.

A crackling spark of jealousy flared up inside me, hot and acrid. Jasher was going to go off into the world now. There was nothing stopping him. He was going to do everything that he'd been dreaming of. What would he find? Who would he meet? I'd be going back to school. In Saltford. I'd be back under Liz's roof, and back in my mundane routine. It was on the tip of my tongue to ask him to take me with him, take me away from my life. We could explore the world together.

"Is your phone nearby?" he said.

I blinked, and visions of backpacking through Nepal with him vaporized. "What?"

"Your phone. Do you have it?"

"That is the last thing I ever expected you to say," I said.

He laughed. "It's important."

I leaned away from him and grabbed my phone from my bedside table. I handed it to him. "I thought you hated cell phones."

"I do, but I need to show you something." He took the phone and turned it on. Then he handed it back to me. "Can you open your photos? It was hard enough for me to figure out how to find your camera. I'll be damned if I can find where the pictures go."

Bemused, I opened my photos. The first photo that popped up made me blink to clear my vision and then stare so hard my eyes misted up. It was me. But it wasn't me.

"So that's why you had my phone in your hand," I said, as I stared.

"Aye. Turns out phones have their uses after all."

I was standing barefoot on the earth, but dirt covered my legs all the way up to the middle of my shins, as though I had just stepped out of a hole. My arms were opened and my fingers splayed. It almost looked like I was directing an orchestra. My face was serene, my mouth was open as though I was speaking. My hair blew out from my head in all directions, like there was a wild wind, but my clothing was limp. It was the eyes that really nailed me, though. They were completely white and aglow with a pure, ethereal light. I looked like an avenging and righteous angel. "That's what I looked like?"

"It is," he said, looking over my shoulder at the image. He kissed the curve of my shoulder and then propped his chin on it.

"I didn't turn into a tree?"

He laughed and lifted his head. "A tree?" He brushed my hair away from my neck. "No. Why, is that what it felt like?"

I nodded. "It felt like I was towering above the whole scene, with big heavy arms that moved slowly, like tree branches. My roots felt like they went a mile into the earth."

"You never looked like a tree, and you didn't move slowly, but I could believe you had roots." He put his lips against my shoulder again.

"What did I sound like? Did I speak, or was that just in my head?"

"No, you did. You sounded like thunder. It was beautiful." The way he said thunder, like t'under, made me smile.

I turned the phone off and set it on the bedside table. I snuggled down into the covers and Jasher lay down behind me, curling an arm over my waist. He pulled me against his chest, fitting me to him, and kissed behind my ear. And just like that, sleep took us.

CHAPTER 35

My cell phone ringing jarred us both awake. I groped for it on the nightstand, unable to open my eyes; they felt glued shut.

"Hello?" I croaked.

"Georjayna?" The voice was urgent and familiar, but it took me several seconds to register who it was.

"Denise?" Why was my mother's secretary calling me? Let alone calling me at the ungodly hour of... I looked at the screen through a barely cracked lid. Oh. It was 8:27. I did some quick math in my head and sat up as I realized that it was five in the morning in Saltford. Jasher sat up beside me, rubbing his eyes.

"Yes, it's Denise. Georjayna, your mother hasn't been well." Her voice was clipped, almost reproachful. "She needs you to come home. I've already changed your flight and emailed your ticket..."

I still had another two weeks before I was scheduled to come home. It began to sink in that Liz must be in a bad way. I threw my legs over the side of the bed, fully awake now.

"You need to be at the airport in six hours. Can you do that for me?"

"Of course," I said. "But what's wrong? It sounds serious." The fear was back with a vengeance. All the normal irritation I felt toward Liz was hiding in a cupboard somewhere. Now all I felt was panic crawling up my throat like a big nasty spider with hooked claws.

Jasher was up and standing on the other side of the bed, his hair sticking up every which way. He was staring at me, eyes wide and hands out, like he didn't know what to do and didn't know what was going on.

"The doctors haven't been able to identify it, so they're doing a few more tests. I don't want you to panic. I'll pick you up at the airport and take you right to the hospital," Denise was saying.

At the word 'hospital' I stopped completely, staring at Jasher. I purposefully closed my eyes. "Hospital?" I repeated.

"She's alright, Georjie. Just focus on getting yourself home, and I'll explain everything. As much as I can, anyway. Talk to you soon." She hung up the phone. This was Denise's way of keeping control, she ends things when she wants to end them. It was the same thing my mother did.

"Georjie." Jasher voice broke through and I opened my eyes.

I am not going to panic.

"It's Liz, she's sick. I have to go home. Can you take me to the train station as soon as I'm ready?"

"Of course." He came around the bed and took me in his arms. His warmth and strength enfolded me. He smelled like trees and sleep. I allowed myself a moment of solace as his hug calmed me. "Did they tell you what's wrong with her? Is she in danger?"

"I don't think so." My voice broke. Guilt was beginning its slow burn, like acid being pumped through my heart and into my veins. I scrolled through my emails, finding the new ticket Denise had sent. "It was my mom's secretary. She didn't tell me much. I have to pack, my plane leaves from Dublin at two forty-five."

"I'll take you to Dublin, Georjie. There's no way I'll let you take the train." Jasher was bending over, peering under the bed.

"But, you have work. What are you doing?"

He pulled out my luggage and put it on the bed, opening it up. "I'm my own boss, I work when I want," he said. "You pack, I'll make us breakfast for the road."

My eyes found his face and I saw there, my own feelings mirrored. We weren't ready for this, to say good-bye. There was a heavy silence as everything that had happened this summer, and especially the day before, filled the space between us.

"I'm here for you Georjie, always," Jasher finally said. "Even if I'm making a pilgrimage to a temple in the Tibetan mountains, or I'm on a tiny island in the South Pacific, I would drop everything and come to you if you asked me to."

I would never ask him to do something like that, but the sentiment made my lower lip wobble. "Does that mean you're going to get a cell phone?" I asked, my eyes misting up in spite of myself.

"A satellite phone, if I have to." He gave me a quirky smile. When he saw my eyes filling up, his expression softened. He circled the bed and took my face in his hands. "It'll be all right, you'll see. You can heal your mom of whatever it is anyway. If you can heal me of seeing the dead, there is no ailment too big for you." He rubbed away a tear. "Just focus on getting home, okay? I'll explain everything to Faith."

I nodded. With that, he gave me a kiss and left me to my packing.

CHAPTER 36

The ride to the airport with Jasher was a thoughtful one. He'd made us tuna sandwiches, bagged up some cheese and crackers, and brought a thermos of tea to share. He ate his meal less than an hour into the drive, but I couldn't work up the appetite for food.

"You won't miss this rain," Jasher said, turning on the windshield wipers as moisture spattered lightly against the glass.

"Actually, I don't mind it," I said, zipping my hoody up to my chin. "It's good for the earth."

He agreed, and we grew silent again. The windshield wipers squeaked and the sound of wet road buzzed under the tires. Jasher broke the silence again with, "Why do you think Mailís decided to appear when we were there? According to what you saw, she'd been trapped in that dusty place for decades. Why surface just then?"

"Because I said her name," I replied.

He looked over at me, surprised. "That's all it took?"

"I didn't figure it out until after the fact, because it seemed weird to me too, but all the clues were there. The fae respond to their names - all it took in my dream was to say their names out loud and they breathed on me." I sat up, another clue falling into place. "Emily."

"Who?"

"That night at Eithne," I said, turning to him. "Emily, the blonde girl with the short hair. While she was telling me the history of Eithne, she listed off the names of seven Irish rebels who had died there. I guess the dead respond to their names, too."

"The seven ghosts," added Jasher, as it clicked into place for him, too.

I shuddered. "Thank God she stopped."

"Aye." Jasher gave his own involuntary shiver of horror. "I'm glad I don't have to deal with that anymore."

"Me too. I hope it sticks."

"It will," he said. Then looked at me a moment later. "Why, you think it won't?"

"I'm sure it will," I added quickly. I hated the look of fear in his eyes. "I'm just… new at this. I don't know how it all works."

"Would be nice if you could find someone like you to talk to," he said. "Like an Obi-Wan of Wise… people."

I smiled and nodded. We fell silent again.

When my bags had been checked and we were saying goodbye in front of security, Jasher got a look of wonderment on his face.

"So, if the fae respond to their names, and Mailís responded to her name, and she was a Wise, and you're a Wise…"

I thought I knew where he was going with this and I started to shake my head.

"Doesn't it stand to reason that you could be called by name, too?"

I laughed. "And what? Materialize out of the air? I don't think so."

"Maybe not out of the air, no. But out of the earth? You did some crazy stuff with the soil, Georjie. You moved huge chunks of it in less than a minute, it was like watching tectonic plates shift in fast-forward. It would have taken men with earth-moving equipment weeks to do what you did."

"How does that mean I could travel through it?"

"It doesn't, I'm just saying, you're a Wise now, it makes you related to the fae, doesn't it? And they came to you when you called them."

"Well, you can try it," I said with a laugh. "While you're on Bora-

Bora drinking young coconuts and swinging in a hammock, you give me a shout and I'll do my best to pop up out of the beach."

He laughed, kissed me sweetly on the lips, and took me in his arms for a long good-bye hug. "I just might do that, Georjie. I just might."

CHAPTER 37

"Mom!" I cried, and I crossed the hospital room to her bedside. She had an IV in her arm. The hair at her temples was streaked with gray. Her cheeks were hollow and the bones in her hands were so horrifyingly visible that I choked back a sob. I leaned over and wrapped my arms around her thin frame. She stroked my back feebly.

"There's a word I haven't heard in a while," she said, softly. Her voice was that of an old woman's.

"Why didn't you call me sooner?" I pulled back to look at her. The words were no sooner out of my mouth than I felt like garbage. She *had* called me, but I hadn't wanted to listen to her, all I could hear were the voices of my own anger. "I'm so sorry." Movement by the door drew my attention. "Denise, would you give us some privacy, please?" I said. "Thank you for picking me up."

Denise gave a curt nod and a tight smile and closed the door behind herself.

"What do they say is wrong?" I sat in the chair near the bed and pulled it close to her.

"Mostly dehydration and accelerated ageing," she said, laying her head back on the pillow. "Doc says I've been working myself to death."

That rang true, but I knew it wasn't all that was at play here. "When did you first notice it?"

"To be honest, the first time I felt like something was wrong was that day I called you and asked how things were going with Jasher." She dabbed at her nose with a tissue.

My fingers grew cold and a chill swept over me. "Go on."

"It was the strangest thing. After we said good-bye, I had to sit down. I felt out of breath, and my mouth was so dry. It seemed like no amount of water could slake my thirst. It was bad for a few hours, and then I seemed to be okay again."

I nodded, taking a deep breath.

"I never felt perfect after that, but I felt a bit better, so I went on working."

"Did you tell anyone?" I already knew the answer. Liz wouldn't voluntarily go to the hospital unless she'd cut off a limb.

"No," she waved a hand. "You know how I am."

"And then?"

"Then, when you and I had that awful fight..."

I closed my eyes to steel myself against what I knew was coming. I had done this to her, without even realizing it.

"I collapsed. It was the strangest thing. I was desperate to speak with you, there was so much to say, but I couldn't do anything but wheeze. Poor Denise just about had a heart attack."

"Why didn't you call me back?"

"Denise rushed me to the hospital, and making another call right away wasn't the priority. Besides, it sounded like you had things going on that were important."

"Oh, Mom," I whispered. I had done this to her. The dangerous side of my powers had been fully demonstrated to me through Mailís, but a new realization had hit me. I could hurt someone without even intending to, just by how I was feeling toward them. "Can you walk?"

"Yes, I can walk," she said. "I'm feeling worlds better than I was."

"Let's go for a walk, want to? Is there a garden nearby?"

She gave me a baffled look. "There is, in the courtyard. It's quite pretty. I'm not sure I'm up for it."

"I'll help you. You'll feel better afterwards, Mom. I promise."

She got out of bed and wrapped a robe around her pyjamas. I found her sandals and toed them into place so she could put them on. She had to take her IV with her, so I rolled it along with us out the door and to the elevator. My mom didn't walk fast, but she wasn't stiff or ungainly, either. The hall was quiet, and I was thankful Denise had disappeared.

As we walked, I asked, "Why did you want me to come home early so badly? Before you got sick, I mean. Was it really that you just missed me?"

Her eyes flashed up at me and back down at the floor. "I did. You know what they say, you don't know what you've got until it's gone."

There was more. I waited for it.

"I was afraid," she finally added, as we stood in front of the elevator.

"Of what?"

"Of you spending too much time at that place."

Now we were getting somewhere. "Where? Sarasborne?"

She took a crushed tissue from the pocket of her robe and dabbed her nose with it. She nodded, not looking me in the eye.

The elevator dinged and the doors swept open. We shuffled inside and I pushed the button for the ground floor.

"What's wrong with Sarasborne, Mom?" I asked.

"It sounds crazy," she said, flatly.

"Try me."

"Your great-grandfather Syracuse was very unusual. He believed in faeries, you know."

"Really?" I bit my cheek to hide my smile.

"He was always on about the fae, drawing pictures of them, telling stories about how special Sarasborne and our family was to them. How they were on the lookout for someone worthy of their gifts."

The little hairs on my forearms stood up. I didn't know if Syracuse had pegged the fae's intentions quite right, but it was even more startling to hear my mother talk like this.

"How come you never told me about any of this before? Especially before I went to Ireland?"

"Well, it's all hogwash," Liz said. "I didn't want to fill your head with all that nonsense."

I hated to challenge her, but I had to know. "If you don't believe it, then why were you scared?"

She looked uncomfortable. The elevator stopped and we stepped out into a hallway bright with windows. Mom directed us to turn left.

"I started to get these feelings," she said, very quietly. "Like something bad might happen to you."

"Like it did to Mailís?" I added, watching her face closely.

Her eyes flashed to mine and stayed there. "Faith told you about her?"

I shook my head. "I found her diary in the library."

The little spots of color in my mother's cheeks faded. "She went crazy, poor thing. Suddenly going on about the fae, the way Syracuse did. And then the suicide." She wrung the tissue in her hands. "I got a bout of superstition," she admitted, her voice going scratchy. "With me not feeling well, and thinking that you were over there where all that strange history...."

"I'm okay, Mom. You don't need to worry."

"I can see that, and I'm sorry, I should have left you there to enjoy the rest of the summer. I just got consumed by my own mental whirlpool." She shook her head. "It's not a good thing for someone in my position, being superstitious. I thought I'd dealt with all that. I must be getting old."

I smiled and shook my head. "You're not getting old, Mom."

I pushed open a door and we walked out into the hospital's sunny courtyard. There weren't many people out enjoying the sunshine, just a man and a woman. The man sat in a wheelchair, his head tilted back and his eyes closed. The woman sat on a bench nearby, reading a book.

I took my mother onto the grass and slipped off my shoes. Tingles swept up my legs as I planted my bare feet against the earth. The feeling of roots shooting out of my soles and into the earth was there, but this time it was slow and lazy, and it didn't trip me. The roots retracted as I lifted my feet from the earth, and extended when I stepped down. The vegetation around me glowed with soft light.

"What are you doing? You hate walking in bare feet. You've hated it since you were little." My mother's eyebrows shot up.

"Try it," I said. "It feels glorious. It's something I learned to like while I was in Ireland."

She slipped off her sandals and stepped onto the grass. "I haven't done this since I was child," she murmured. She had two bunions, one at the base of each big toe.

I took her hand. "Isn't it nice? Close your eyes."

She closed her eyes and tilted her face up to the sun.

I let the healing powers flow through me, up my legs, into my torso, down my arm and into her hand. It was easier now than it was before, like removing a dam and just letting the water flow.

"Oh," my mom said, startled. "Oh, Georjie!"

"It's all right," I whispered.

"It feels wonderful." She laughed out loud and the man in the wheelchair looked over at us. I let the healing power overflow and reach out toward him and the woman. I didn't direct it with intention, I just let it go where it wanted, like flowing liquid.

I watched as my mother's skin plumped out, her hair lost its brittle texture, and the gray at her roots filled in with blond. The skin on the back of her hands thickened and turned from translucent to opaque. The bunions on her feet shrank and her toe bones straightened. My eyebrows shot up as I watched the IV needle push out of her skin, the tape pulled away from her as the adhesive could no longer hold. The needle fell out and dangled from the IV tower.

Eventually, the healing energy stopped moving so much. It sort of swirled and drifted through me, then became slow and lazy.

"How do you feel?" I asked

She opened her eyes. "What did you do?"

"I learned a trick or two, in Ireland," I said. "Don't let it alarm you."

She gazed at me thoughtfully. Her eyes misted and she pulled me into a hug. "I am so sorry, Georjie."

"What?" I blinked, startled. "No, Mom. I am. I mean, neither of us has been perfect, but I… I'll never bulldoze you like that again."

She shook her head and pulled back. "I've been so absent. Ever since your father left, I haven't known what to do. All I knew was work. I thought that if I didn't let myself think, or feel..." She touched a hand to my cheek. "If I didn't let myself love you, then I wouldn't be hurt when you left home the way I was when your father left." She shook her head. "I know they're not the same thing at all. What an idiot I've been. What a mistake. We've lost so many years, living like ships passing in the night."

"Let's not lose anymore, Mom."

She shook her head. "No. No more. Can you forgive me?" Tears ran freely down her face now.

"Forgiveness is easy when you realize that you aren't perfect, either."

It was a start. I'm not going to tell you that everything has been just hunky-dory for me and my mom ever since that day. We still argue, we still get on each other's nerves, and I'm still trying to figure out how to feel ticked off without letting my emotion turn my powers on. It's getting easier. And yes, I put into motion the changing of my name from Sutherland to Sheehan.

The doctor, a distracted looking man with a comb-over and thick glasses, discharged my mom later that day, pronouncing her fully recovered. Denise was happy, but she looked at me askance more than once, like she thought something smelled funny. I never explained anything to her, and I don't think my mom has either. It's good that she works for my mom, so she's not permitted to be nosy.

Because none of my friends were home from their adventures yet, Mom booked some time off work and we've been having a bit of a staycation. That's how I've been able to pen these memoirs. I guess I'll leave them for now. Close them up. I still have a lot of searching to do about who I am and what I've become. Maybe, when I know more, I'll write more.

You might think that my mom would grill me about what happened, but she didn't. Even though we've begun mending the bridge between us, it's still foreign to bare our souls to one another. One step at a time.

I called my Aunt Faith to thank her and to say goodbye. I didn't tell her any of what happened, either. For now, it's a secret between Jasher and me. I didn't know what Brendan thought, but I decided to let Jasher handle that. We've spoken a couple of times. He is going to help his father rebuild his home, he says the O'Brien property is already full of plantlife. He's also planning a trip around the world. He doesn't waste time. We tossed around the idea of me joining him next summer, after graduation. I get a little overexcited when I think about it.

After I said goodbye to Faith, I passed the phone over to my mom.

That was an hour ago. They're still talking.

CHAPTER 38

I saved my work, closed my laptop and went through the house to the kitchen. I made myself some tea and took it with me through the patio doors and into the back yard. The moon was full and her soft light dusted everything, illuminating Saltford with her cool magic.

I closed the screen door behind me and walked down our garden path in my flip flops to the fire pit. I sat in one of our hand-made Adirondack chairs and listened to the crickets chirp. Only two months ago I was sitting in this exact place, only I was moaning about leaving my friends and having to go to Ireland for the summer. I was complaining about Liz and her ignorance about me and my life, the ravine between us. I looked out over the ocean, the sparkling lights along the harbor. They didn't call our neighborhood Bella Vista for nothing.

I kicked off my flip flops and curled my toes in the cool grass. Immediately, the life force of the vegetation and soil around me glowed with colored light. It was soft, and every species pulsed gently with its own rhythm. I knew them all by name now, just like I knew the fae.

My eye was drawn by a brighter, harder light coming from the harbor. I stood and walked to the crest of the hill at the end of our yard.

A line of bright, almost harsh light made its way under houses and roads and down to the harbor. The illuminated line went into the water, glowed blue as it lit up the ocean, and continued on toward the horizon. It grew dimmer and dimmer as it descended into the depths of the Atlantic, until it finally disappeared from sight.

My heart sped up as my eyes followed the same line of light in the other direction. I turned, my gaze following it underneath Saltford and straight west. My breath hitched when I saw another thick glowing line intersect with the first one. They crossed, making a perfect intersection with ninety degree angles at each corner. The light at the intersection appeared so bright that it swallowed up whole buildings. Every tree, shrub, and blade of grass growing in the path of this line was shining like a supernova. The second line ran south and north as far as my eyes could see. Third and fourth lines, these ones not quite as bright as the other two, intersected and passed through the point where the other brightest two crossed. The slightly dimmer ones ran north-east and south-west, and north-west and south-east.

"Ley lines," I whispered. Goosebumps rose on my arms and neck as the night breeze stirred my hair. Saltford had been built on four ley lines, and they intersected right under my high school. The large brick building was so swallowed by light that I could barely make out its shape. How many times had I looked down from the crest of this very hill, at that very building, and never seen the ley lines? Did anyone else know they were there?

What was it Faith had said about them? Her words came back to me in broken echoes.

An undetectable matrix of energy lines criss-crossing the earth...

Linking sites of supernatural significance...

Rich with electromagnetic power...they attract supernatural activity...

My eyes followed the brightest ley line again, out into the Atlantic, down into the water. Its light turned blue as it submerged and then faded away into the horizon, heading due East. Where did it go? All the way around the earth? What else had been built on top of this same ley line? What did it connect Saltford to?

I looked back at my high school, barely visible against the bright light. I toed my way back into my flip-flops, putting a barrier between the soles my feet and the earth. Immediately, the ley line disappeared.

What did it mean for a school full of teenagers to be spending most of their days in a building that had been erected right on top of intersecting ley lines? What did it mean for Saltford?

EPILOGUE

Targa: *How's things with the cuzball?*

Me: *I'll keep him. But I'm pretty sure we'll never think of one another as cousins.*

Saxony: *Holy change of tone. What happened?*

Me: *We got close.*

Targa: *How close, exactly?*

Me: *A story best told in person.*

Saxony: *That's mean!*

Me: *Well neither of you two have coughed up any gory details!*

Saxony: *Good point.*

Me: *I'm home now. I'm waiting for you with bated breath.*

Targa: *So early? How come?*

Me: *My mom hasn't been well. She'll be okay though.*

Saxony: *You have a mom? I thought you just lived with a roommate named Liz?*

Me: *Turns out we're related. Either of you two know what's going on with Akiko?*

Saxony: *I think she's gone underground for some Japanese crime syndicate. We may never hear from her again.*

Targa: *As long as she puts the crime on hold long enough to be at our sleepover...*

<<<<>>>>

AFTERWORD & ACKNOWLEDGMENTS

Still with me? Sweet! So you've read all that, and now you're reading this, too! Thank you! I hope you enjoyed Born of Earth, it was a special challenge for me. When I was 18, I took a year off to travel and Ireland is where I set my sights. I learned to dance there (Irish style, of course) and consequently performed with an Irish troupe in Canada for ten years after that.

Ireland holds a special place in my heart, not just because I have ancestry there, but because I find the culture beautiful and fascinating. I spent many summers enjoying the Celtic Roots Festival in Goderich, Ontario, and for much of my teens and twenties, life didn't seem complete without Celtic music and dance. I've since visited many other countries, and haven't been back to Ireland in almost twenty years, but its mythology and history have never let me go. As I pen this little blurb at the end of the journey Born of Earth took me on, I find myself itching to visit the Emerald Isle once again.

Thank you to my family, my tirelessly supportive parents, Gene & Victoria, to my brothers and their families; your support does wonders for me. To my Beta Readers whose eagle-eyes don't let me get away with anything, and whose feedback never ceases to make my stories better. To my Editor, Teresa Hull, who has been such a joy to work with and who has somehow made time for me in her busy schedule, even sometimes on short notice - thank you! Most importantly to my readers, whose kind words and supportive feedback give me the juice I need to keep writing.

I learn so much every time I write a book, and I know that I'll only continue to get better and better at my chosen craft. If you enjoyed Born of Earth, please consider writing a review. You have no idea how much honest and fair reviews do for authors like me. Really! No bones about it!

Thank you to Lora, Virginio, Patch and Alex, for being my family in Italy, and nurturing me in my creative endeavours. Thank you to my cheering group of friends and the friends I have met through this author journey.

On to the Born of Æther excerpt. I hope you enjoy! If you'd like to be notified whenever I release a story (which I try to do once a month, whether its a short story, novella, full novel, or anthology) please sign up for my newsletter at alknorrbooks.com or join me on Facebook at @alknorrbooks

Catchya later! A.L. Knorr

EXCERPT FROM BORN OF ÆTHER

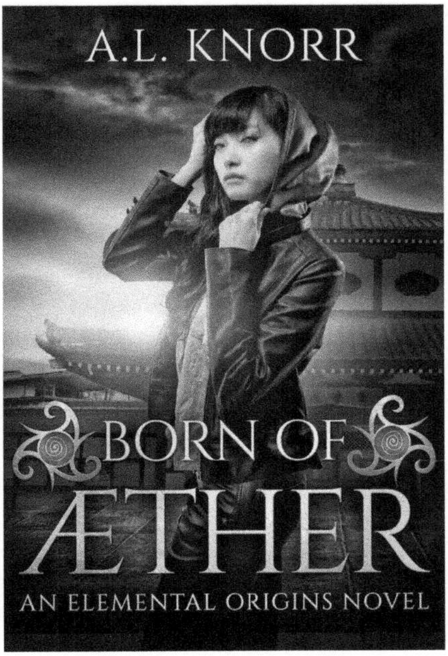

They say if you tell a lie long enough, you'll eventually believe it, but Akiko will never forget who she really is.

Akiko Susumu is not what she seems. Her life as a normal teen living in a coastal Canadian town is a complete sham. The old man she lives with is not her grandfather, he's her captor. And Akiko isn't a teen. In fact, she isn't even human.

But Akiko isn't allowed to share the reality of her true nature with a single soul. Not even her three best friends know of the power she could wield, given the chance.

So, when she's sent back to her homeland to steal an ancient samurai sword, she jumps at the chance to secure her freedom, only to get caught in a deadly game of cat and mouse with the most dangerous crime syndicate in Japan.

Can Akiko escape with her life and her soul, or is true freedom as elusive as the Aether she was born from?

Turn the page to read a sneak peek of Born of Aether!

PROLOGUE

The moans of the wounded and the dying filled the narrow valley. The full moon, big and bright and already high in the sky, cast its cold blue light over the battle scene. Long thin shadows from arrows and spears embedded in the earth and in flesh slanted across grass, mud, and dark pools of blood. Crows gathered in the branches of nearby trees, their throaty screams alerting other scavengers from miles around. A few brave birds descended to the mud between the bodies, preparing to pick apart their dinner and usher the dead toward the slow transition into dust.

The dark shape of a small black fox darted from the trees to skirt the perimeter of the battlefield. Sniffing the air and stopping to listen, she salivated heavily at the smell of hot blood still pumping from the veins of the dying. At the sound of a moan she bolted into the shadows, her movements quick and sure-footed. She cocked her ears toward the sound, and moved swiftly to investigate.

A dying warrior lay face up to the ghostly moon. Shallow breaths lifted his armored chest with the quiet creak of leather and clink of chainmail. A dark pool gathered between his left arm and his torso as his life poured from his body and soaked into the earth.

The small fox approached on silent paws, stopping to listen before taking a few more steps. Her head low and her ears forward, she inched up to the still-warm and fragrant pool of blood. As a long and final sigh escaped the samurai, her pink tongue darted out to taste the vitamin-rich liquid, the death of one passing on life to another in a cycle as old as the earth itself.

When the fox had raised eight litters, killed and eaten a thousand rodents, escaped a hundred predators, and seen the snows go and the rains come a dozen times, her weak and aged body crawled into a familiar hollow under a juniper for the last time.

The flesh and bone of the samurai whose blood sustained her all those years ago had long since returned to the earth. The memory of that battlefield faded from her fox mind, a nearly insignificant event in her short life. There was room only for the present moment, for the death stealing into her bones and making her shiver.

She settled into her hollow, curling her thick tail over her paws and in front of her nose. She watched the light of another full moon through the thick needles of the bush as her breathing grew shallow and short. She knew what was coming, and she faced it alone, unafraid, and without self-pity. She was tired. She let out a long sigh and her ribs sank as she surrendered.

On any normal day with any normal fox, those ribs would not rise again. But life gives way to life, and as the earthly fox dies, the spirit of the samurai warrior awakens, and the ribs do rise again.

CHAPTER 1

Is there a limit to how many lies one person can tell? My life was so saturated with them that I was afraid to open my mouth for fear of ensnaring myself in one of Grandfather's falsehoods. They say that if you tell a lie for long enough, you'll eventually come to believe it. But that would never happen to me. It couldn't. I would never forget who I was, where I came from, and what had happened to me. It didn't matter how many lies Grandfather commanded me to tell, or what ridiculous story he had dripping from my lips to protect himself. I would always know the truth, and he couldn't change that.

The truth.

The truth was not that I was his granddaughter. I was his captive.

The truth was not that my family died in a plague that swept our village. I had been taken from my home against my will.

The truth was not that my mother was Japanese and my father was Canadian. Both of my parents were Japanese. Grandfather made up the lie to fabricate some connection to this land, to explain our presence in this country.

The truth was not that I was a sixteen-year-old girl. I was nearly a century old.

The truth was not that I was human. I just looked like it.

I disliked walking home alone after school because these were the thoughts that most often clutched my mind. Normally, I walked home with Saxony every day, since we lived in the same neighborhood. But today she had a phone interview with the au pair agency she had applied with, so after saying goodbye to Targa and Georjayna, I had left Saltford High on my own.

Though it was April, the weather was bitterly cold and gray. Snow and ice crusted the streets and bare branches reached up to condemn the cloudy sky.

The suburb we lived in was quiet today. Very few cars passed me, and no one walked the sidewalks. It was too miserable outside for playing, and the playground I passed was abandoned.

Our bungalow was the second to last house on our street. Even from a distance it looked unwelcome. The windows were dark and the curtains drawn. I walked up our front yard, stepped up onto our small deck, and entered our coatroom.

"I'm home," I called out in Japanese as I kicked off my boots. I pulled on my slippers and hung my parka on its hook.

"Akiko," came Grandfather's voice from the small front room.

I poked my head around the corner. "I'm here," I repeated. "Need anything?"

"Sit," Grandfather said, gesturing to the couch across from his chair. His laptop was open and it sent a blue glow onto his lined face.

I frowned. When Grandfather asked me to sit, it usually meant he had something more complicated for me to do. He hadn't asked me to sit in years. Most of my commands these days were mere errands—groceries, translating something for him, mailing something at the post office, making dinner, doing laundry, cleaning the house, shoveling the front walk. I was the world's most exotic house keeper.

I sat and waited.

He steepled his withered hands and gazed at me from across the coffee table. "My name is Daichi Hotaka," he said.

My mouth dropped open. I could do nothing but stare. My heart began to pound. Something was going to change, something had happened. My mind raced. What had happened? Why, after all this time, was he finally telling me his name? My hands instantly felt ice-cold. I didn't know what to say, so all I did was wait, skin prickling with anticipation. With effort, I closed my mouth.

"I have been searching for something that was stolen from me many years ago." Nothing about his countenance changed, but I could sense a vibration of excitement about him that I had never felt before. "I have finally found it."

He reached a hand out and spun the laptop to face me.

My eyes dropped to the screen. It showed a video on YouTube entitled 'Ryozen Museum to Display Artifacts from the Bakamatsu Period. Early summer.' My eyes scanned the text below the video: *The Ryozen Museum of History in Kyoto, Japan, specializes in the history of the Bakumatsu period and the Meiji Restoration. The museum is dedicated to the often violent events that brought an end to the Tokugawa regime at the climax of the Edo Period.*

Daichi had frozen the screen on a closeup of a wooden rack carrying four samurai short swords. Three of them were in black sheaths, and one of them was in a blue sheath with some kind of pattern on it. He pointed a twisted finger at the short sword with the blue sheath. It looked like the design on the sheath might be of trees, but the screen was blurry so it was difficult to make out.

"Bring me this wakizashi," he said.

My eyes widened and flew to his face. Had I heard him correctly? I swallowed hard, my mind a torrent of questions. This was more than just an errand. This was a mission, and probably an illegal one. "It is in Kyoto, Grandfather," I said. "You want me to go back to Japan?" A torrent of emotions crashed through me like a tsunami. After all this time, he was going to let me visit our homeland? Alone? We hadn't been back in Japan since we left over a lifetime ago – me caged and in the form of a bird. Grandfather had never expressed a desire to go back, but then again, he rarely expressed desires more complex than hunger. I had long ago given up hope of setting foot in Japan again.

He nodded. "It will be on display soon, and not for very long." He placed his hands flat on his thighs and leaned forward. "The time for this is now. I have spent years looking for this sword. We may never have another chance."

"I am to—" I paused, processing his command and what it meant. "Steal it?"

His eyes gleamed and he stared at me unblinking. He took a long slow breath and each moment that passed raised gooseflesh on my skin. "You bring me this wakizashi, and I will give you your freedom."

* * *

My head was still spinning a few days later. I sat through my classes in a daze, and avoided spending too much time with Saxony since even she was bound to notice my distraction. Every night I lay awake praying that Daichi wasn't playing some kind of sick joke on me, that he wouldn't retract his offer. I had chosen to walk home alone every day so I could think. If I kept this up, Saxony was going to chase me down.

I scuffed my feet along the sidewalk, kicking chips of ice skittering down the pavement. This had to be my last solitary stroll home, and thankfully the shock had worn off enough that I thought I could hang out with my friends without alerting them that something big was happening.

Daichi barked at me from the kitchen as soon as I stepped into the house. "Akiko?"

"Here," I called, taking off my jacket and boots. My heart leapt into my throat and I fought to wrestle my irrational dread back into its place. Just because he had something to say didn't mean he was going to withdraw the offer. I took a breath, put my hat and mitts into the wooden bin under the coatrack, and pulled on my slippers. I padded down the hall to the kitchen and immediately began to warm up. Daichi kept the heat cranked up no matter the season.

He sat at the kitchen table staring out into our snow-covered back yard. A small cardboard box sat on the table in front of him. He looked at me as I entered.

"Sit."

I sat, heart pounding in my ears, and pleading inside that he wasn't about to rescind his offer.

He pushed the cardboard box across the table toward me. "You will need this."

I stifled an audible sigh of relief. He was furnishing me with some kind of necessity, not calling the whole thing off. I slid the box closer and opened it. Unfolding the tissue paper revealed black fabric. Bemused, I pulled out the fabric and held it out. It was so soft and thin that it slipped through my fingers like air. Dangling it by the top, I could finally see what it was. It had short sleeves and the body of it was so short I doubted that it would even come to my knees.

"A bathrobe, Grandfather?" On Georjayna, it wouldn't even cover her butt. "Uh... thank you."

I spotted a small bulge in the pocket on the front of the robe. I fished out a pair of thin slippers in the same material. As footwear, they would fall apart within days. I couldn't help my look of confusion.

"They are one hundred percent silk," Daichi said matter-of-factly.

"Oh?"

He took the robe from me and got to his feet stiffly. He brushed the cardboard box to the side and lay the robe out flat on the table. He spread the arms out in a perfect 'T', tucked the slippers into the front pocket and began to roll the robe from the bottom up. Folding it over and over into a stripe of fabric no thicker than an inch, he picked the length of it up and looped it around my neck twice, snug enough that if he'd pulled it any tighter I might have coughed. He tied the ends in a knot and stepped back.

I looked up at him, fingering the odd scarf. Was the old man finally losing his mind? I swallowed and felt the silk tighten.

"Grandfather," I began. "I'm confused."

"Become a bird," he said.

When he gave me an order, I could no more hold back the tide than I could prevent myself from executing it. I phased into a small gray chicken, my clothing falling past my small feathered body to the floor. I landed on the edge of my chair and almost slipped off the smooth wooden seat. I squawked and flapped, my claws scrabbling for purchase. The silk loosened from around my neck but it stayed draped around my chicken shoulders.

"Become a bird that can fly," Daichi barked with exasperation.

I phased into a crow and hopped up on the table, tilting my head at Daichi. The silk robe hung from my neck like an absurd scarf, but I could barely feel its weight.

Daichi opened our back door and a burst of cold air swept the kitchen. "Fly to the ocean and return," he commanded. "Do not lose the silk!"

I hopped to the edge of the table, hooked my claws over the rim, and took off through the open door. I dropped low toward the ground, picked up a gust of wind and swooped upward. Up and up I spiraled, the silk hanging from my neck in front of my wings. I didn't feel the cold nearly as much when I was a bird, and the wind increased as I approached the ocean. I swept out over the beach, cawing my pleasure hoarsely at this brief freedom. I circled over the waves and headed back to the house. Well-kept yards covered in snow swept by beneath me as I passed over our suburb.

The back door to our kitchen opened and I slowed down and flew inside.

"Go to your room and become human," came the next order.

I whooshed past Daichi, landed in the hall, and hopped into my bedroom. I beaked the door closed and phased back into my human form. I stood there naked in front of the full-length mirror, my chest rising and falling as I caught my breath. The silk robe was once again tight around my throat.

Daichi had put my clothes on my bed. I pulled them on and went back to the kitchen where he was once again seated at the table, waiting.

His eyes, deep in their wrinkled folds, dropped to the black silk around my neck. "It stayed," he said.

"Yes."

"Still confused?" he asked, folding his gnarled fingers on the table and leaning forward.

"A little." I sat down across from him. "I understand you want me to have clothing for when I arrive in Japan, but—"

"It will not disappear," he said, cutting me off. "It will not disappear in the Æther."

I frowned. I wanted to ask him how he could know that for sure, but I knew what the answer would be. The same it always was, the non-answer.

Daichi leaned forward and patted the back of my hand in a rare moment of contact. He gave me the non-answer anyway. "I was old before I met you," he said. He got up and walked in his slow plodding way toward the living room where he would wait until our evening meal was ready.

"What do you want for dinner, Grandfather?" I asked. "Besides rice."

He paused and looked back. Amusement was just a ghost at his lips, but the upward twitch of his mouth was unmistakable. "Chicken." He disappeared around the corner.

I smiled and untied the knot of silk at my throat. Funny how after so many years together, even under unhappy circumstances, there could still be some kind of humor between us.

CHAPTER 2

Saxony closed her locker and pulled her hood up over her wild curls. She hooked her arm through mine. "Come on, I'll walk you home. It's been too long." She eyed the gloomy sky outside. "Why did I put away my winter stuff? It was so nice last week."

"You always put it away too early," I said, smiling. Every year was the same. "We live near the Atlantic—don't you know by now that spring means snow and freezing rain?"

"Don't swear," she said. She pulled a folded yellow document from her pocket. "Look what I got today." She waved it in front of my face.

"A subpoena?"

"Noooooooooo." She drew out the word with artificial annoyance.

"A parking ticket?"

"No. Stop that."

I gave a fake and exaggerated gasp. "Jury duty?"

Her eyes grew wide and she gasped, too. "How did you know?"

"What?" I gaped at her.

She whacked my shoulder. "No. Shut up and listen, would you?"

"A love letter?" I tried one more time.

"Yes!" She bounced up and down. "From the au pair agency in

Toronto. They have a place for me in Venice. Guess who is spending the summer in bella Italia?"

"No way." I held the school's front door open for her and we walked out into a fine wet mist.

"Way. And I can't get there soon enough," she said, pulling her collar up around her ears. "No one should live here. Brrrrrrrrrr." She shivered. "Would you come visit me there?"

"Uh..." The idea of visiting Saxony in Italy during the summer was heavenly. "Grandfather—"

"I know, I know," she interrupted. "He'll never let you go to Europe. I was completely shocked when he let you sleep over at Georjie's house last year for her birthday. It's the only nice thing he's done for you like, ever. Have I ever told you that I'm not all that fond of your grandfather?"

I smiled and hooked her elbow as we took the concrete steps down to the sidewalk. "A couple of times. Even though you've never met him."

"A," she said, holding up a long finger, "whose fault is that?" She held up a second finger. "And two, I dislike him on principle. He never lets you do anything fun. It's like he's got you on an invisible leash."

I had to smile at her description. It was worse than a leash. I wondered what she'd say if I told her he wasn't my grandfather and that he'd basically stolen my soul. I cleared my throat. I was bound not to say any such thing. Instead, I said, "You might be surprised to learn that he's sending me to Japan."

"He's never once even let you have me over, your best friend—" Saxony continued, but then froze abruptly and pulled me to a stop. "Wait. What?"

Her face had gone even paler than normal, quite an accomplishment for a redhead with a porcelain complexion.

"Not for good," I said quickly. "Just for the summer."

"Really? I stand corrected. What for?"

I gave Saxony the lie that Daichi had told me to say. "He wants me to spend the summer with the Japanese side of my family, since I never knew them. They live in a small village in the mountains on the east side. It's supposed to be beautiful."

Saxony narrowed her eyes and studied my face.

"What?" I tugged on her arm to get her walking again.

"I'm just trying to figure out if you're happy about it." She matched me stride for stride. She gripped my elbow, and didn't take her eyes from my face.

My heart sped up the way it always did when I was under scrutiny, even from those I trusted. Too many lies had passed my lips for me to ever feel completely comfortable with anyone digging for more information. The irony of the situation was that I was dying to tell my story to my friends. What a relief it would be to express the suffering and loss I'd endured. I had been alone in it for so long. I shot Saxony a side eye. "And?"

She studied me intensely.

"Are you okay?" I asked. "You're not blinking."

She gave a sigh. "I gave up trying to read you about a week after meeting you." She relaxed her grip on my elbow. "So, *are* you happy about it? Do you even want to go?"

I shrugged and tried to put a neutral expression on my face. I had become a master at hiding my emotions—from my captor and from my friends. One of the reasons I liked spending time with Saxony was that she usually didn't dig too hard and she talked a lot. She was the extrovert I was safe hiding behind. But as she'd gotten older, she'd gotten better at asking questions.

"It is what it is," I answered.

She groaned. "I hate when you say that. Fine, have it your way." She stepped around a patch of ice and pulled her collar up to her chin again. "Did I tell you that Jack plastic-wrapped the toilet last night? Was *I* that brain-damaged at fifteen?"

As Saxony talked, I relaxed into her world. Her family was so normal, so loving. Hers was a life I could watch from the outside with envy. Georjayna struggled with a mom who didn't care enough, and Targa struggled with a mom she felt responsible for. Only Saxony had the stability of an intact family. I wondered if it was where she got her confidence from. I'd seen her walk into a party where she knew no one and within an hour she knew everyone's name, had endeared some of the girls to herself, and had most of the guys following her around like puppies. She also annoyed some people to no end because she was always talking, laughing, always the center of attention. She was the perfect companion to divert eyes away from me. Saxony, Georjie, and Targa were my first close human friends. They'd become my anchor and the only good thing I had in my captivity. My mind went back to Daichi's words.

Bring me this wakizashi, and I'll give you your freedom.

Freedom.

I had been staring down the barrel of an endless, useless life. Servant to the whims of an elderly Japanese man who should have been dead a hundred years ago and who never shared his motivations with me for any choice he made. Who never told me why he'd brought me here, what he wanted, or how I might move on with my life one day.

Until now.

There was no way Daichi could be happy with our life the way it had become. I had never actually seen him happy. Why anyone as miserable as Daichi would even want to be immortal was beyond me. The waste of it sickened me. It twisted in my stomach and made me want to scream.

Every night for decades, Daichi had me phase into a bird and locked me in a cage. All I wanted at that time was to remain human, to have human dreams again, and sleep in a soft warm bed. Then when he finally let me remain human and had a bed delivered to the house for my room, the nightmares started. He never said anything about my night terrors. He never forced me to go back to my cage. I did that all on my own. The passing of time was easier to bear in bird-form, and I didn't have nightmares. It was a little better now. Sometimes I spent the night in my cage, sometimes in my bed, depending on my mood.

When he enrolled me in school and forced me to spend hours studying English and practicing to eliminate my Japanese accent, it served two purposes. It equipped me to be his go-between in the foreign place he'd moved us to, and it kept me so busy that I fell into bed exhausted and dreamed about grammar instead of that fateful day in the woods when my sister had betrayed and abandoned me.

When I finished the high school on the south side of Saltford, he moved me to a school in the north and started me over again. I was more than three years into my cycle at Saltford High and this time around it was impossible not to ace every class. I had no trace of a Japanese accent left, and the North American way of life had become my way of life. I couldn't allow myself to dream of what I would do if I had my life back. I wondered if Daichi felt even a hint of guilt about keeping a creature as powerful as I was behind bars for his own selfish purpose...whatever that was. A surge of dragonflies spiraled up from my stomach and battered my ribs from the inside when I thought about what little seemed to remain between me and my freedom.

"Hey?" Saxony squeezed my arm.

"What? Sorry." I blinked. We were in front of my house already.

"I said, when do you leave?"

"We haven't booked my ticket yet, but it'll be shortly after the school year ends."

Saxony nodded. "Same time as me. Let's make sure we get the four of us together before you and I go."

"Sure, that would be great."

We said goodbye and I wandered up the cinderblock steps to our bungalow. A shiver of anticipation went through me as I thought about my impending flight. I would be flying, but there was no need to book a plane ticket. I'd be making this journey on my own wings, the wings of one of the few birds that could fly high enough to reach the Æther. Thirty thousand feet up, somewhere in the vicinity of earth's ozone layer, lay the home of all spiritual energy and the force that had made my sister and I each what we were.

Don't miss the next magical tale in The Elemental Origins Series! Visit your country's Amazon store to purchase.

Lightning Source UK Ltd.
Milton Keynes UK
UKHW020951220520
363663UK00012B/2406

9 781775 067146